WARNING

This book contains scenes of intense violence and some disturbing themes. Some parts of this book may be considered violent, cruel, disturbing, or unusual. Many of these scenes feature violence towards high school teenagers. Certain implications may trigger strong emotional responses. This book is *not* intended for those easily offended or appalled. Please enjoy at your own discretion.

Table of Contents

The Social Media Murders

Jon Athan

For more information on this book or the
author, please visit www.jon-athan.com. General
inquiries are welcome.

Facebook:
https://www.facebook.com/AuthorJonAthan
Twitter: @Jonny_Athan
Email: info@jon-athan.com

Book cover by Sean Lowery:
http://highimpactcovers.com

ISBN-13: 978-1547098514
ISBN-10: 1547098511

Thank you for the support!

Chapter One

A Chat

Tiffany Anderson stared at her reflection on the full-length mirror in her bedroom, practically leering at herself like a pretentious pervert. Her red flannel shirt was open, revealing her matching bra and flat stomach. She didn't wear any pants, but the bottom of the shirt covered her underwear. Her blonde hair was tied in a tousled bun, strands protruding every which way.

The room was lit up like a Dario Argento movie. Her bedroom was mainly illuminated by a red neon sign over her dresser. The sign read: *Babe.* On the parallel wall, blue moonlight poured into the room through the window above her bed. The red and blue tones illuminated her figure.

Stroking her ego, the teenager whispered, "You're hot, Tiffany. Damn, you are just gorgeous. How do they resist you? How–"

She stopped upon hearing crackling and snickering sounds. She glanced over at her laptop, which sat on her bed. There were three familiar faces on her screen—her closest friends. She was in the middle of a Skype video chat. Her friends—Melanie Myers, Kyle Webb, and Hailey Washington—chatted and laughed. Their chatter could be heard through her earbuds.

Tiffany huffed, then she shouted, "I'm coming, I'm coming! I'll be right there, idiots!"

She sat on her bed and placed the computer on her lap. As she inserted the earbuds into her ears, she heard her friends and joined the conversation.

She asked, "What are you guys laughing at?"

Kyle, a wavy-haired teenager, responded, "*You,* Tiff. We're laughing at you. We're trying to have a conversation over here and you just walk away to check yourself out. Shit, how conceited can you be?"

"Oh, *please.* I was just checking my hair. You said you were going to get a snack and Hailey had to go check on her grandma. What did you expect me to do? Talk to Melanie?"

Melanie, a baby-faced brunette teenager, said, "Hey! If you're insinuating that I have nothing interesting to say, you're wrong. I'm interesting, okay?"

In a croaky tone, blatantly mocking her, Tiffany grimaced and repeated, "If you're insinuating that I have nothing interesting to say..."

"Bitch..."

The group shared a laugh. Insults were hurled at one another, but the teenagers didn't mind. The bickering was playful.

As she recomposed herself, Hailey, a dark-haired slacker, said, "Okay, let's drop all of that shit-talking for a minute. Seriously, we don't have time for that. We have to talk about the test in Wilson's class. If I fail another one, I fail the entire class. I *can't* fail his class, guys."

"Well, why don't we cheat?" Tiffany suggested, a devilish smirk on her face.

"Okay, *how?* I need the answers, you need the answers, we all need those damn answers. How are we going to cheat?"

Chiming-in, Michael said, "Well, *I* don't need the answers 'cause I don't have that class with you, but I'll tell you what you have to do. Trust me, it's easy, Hailey. You just have to show a little skin. Okay, it might not be easy for you since you have the skin of Freddy Krueger, but if someone else showed him something, he'd be blind for days."

Again, the group laughed. Insulting someone's appearance was easy, surviving the verbal attack was difficult. The high school social life required thick skin, especially when your so-called friends were willing to throw you under the bus for a cheap laugh.

Hailey rolled her eyes and said, "*Whatever.* I'm being serious here. If I don't pass his class, I don't graduate. Good luck buying weed without me. I know you're all too pussy to buy it yourselves, stingy bitches..."

"Whoa, whoa, whoa," the trio of students said in perfect harmony.

Tiffany said, "Don't worry about it, Hailey. Listen, Kyle's right. I'll wear a little skirt, I'll lick my lips a little, and I'll show him some skin. I'll get his attention while you cheat off of Melanie, and Melanie can cheat off of that nerd that sits next to her. It's that easy."

Hailey responded, "Okay, well... I hope it works. I don't know if it's *that* easy. You know, I heard Wilson is messing around with someone from school already."

"Yeah, I've heard about that, too. I think I know that slut. A little disgusting cheerleader who can't keep her paws to herself. Dirty cunt..."

The group became silent upon hearing Tiffany's vile insults. Bickering amongst themselves was normal and accepted—it was part of life. When they spoke about someone without their knowledge, it was personal and hateful. There was a *look* in Tiffany's eyes that frightened the group—an icy glare of hatred.

Changing the subject, Melanie asked, "*Anyway,* have you guys heard about the dead girl?"

"Anna Lee?" Kyle said in an uncertain tone.

"Yeah. You heard about her?"

Tiffany said, "Yeah, *she's dead.*"

Melanie smiled and shook her head. She said, "No, no. I mean, have you heard the new rumors about *how* she died?"

Tiffany furrowed her brow and tilted her head, curious. She was a young, pretty girl, but she had a hidden interest in the macabre.

She asked, "How did she die?"

Melanie explained, "It's crazy. I heard her... her jaw was *ripped* off of her head and her tongue was cut off."

Eww—the girls exclaimed as they listened to the rumor. Meanwhile, Kyle chuckled and shook his head. Despite their reactions, they weren't actually bothered by the gruesome details of a classmate's death. Tears were not shed, prayers were not said.

Melanie continued, "I don't know if it's true, I didn't see it, but it sounded real to me. I mean, there's supposedly a video of it online. They said her parents couldn't stop crying when they went in to identify her body, too. They found her jaw, but they never found her tongue. It's some crazy shit."

As she stared down at her keyboard, Tiffany said, "Well, maybe Anna had a big mouth and someone wanted to shut her up. Maybe everything she–"

Thud—Tiffany stopped upon hearing a sound. She glanced over her shoulder and stared at the doorway. The sound of creaky wood and rattling windows entered her room from the hallway. The noise would be normal on any other day, but she was home alone. Everything caused suspicion.

Noticing the fear on her face, Kyle smiled and asked, "What's wrong with you, Tiff? You look like you just saw a ghost. Maybe it was Anna's ghost..."

"No. I... I think I heard something."

"Now that you mention it, I thought I saw someone walking behind you. Yeah, there was someone in your hallway. I'd be careful if I were you."

"Fuck off, Kyle," Tiffany responded without taking her eyes off of the doorway. She glanced back at the screen and said, "I'll be right back. I'm going to go check it out."

***

Tiffany pulled the earbuds out of her ears, then she walked out of her room. She found herself in the hallway. The doors to the left and right were closed. She walked down the hall until she approached the front side of the home. To her left, an archway led to the kitchen. The spacious living room resided to her right. The front door waited directly in front of her.

She approached the door and checked the locks. The latch lock was still secured. She peeked through the peephole. Her parents' car was nowhere in sight.

She flicked a switch near the archway and illuminated the kitchen. An incessant *humming* sound emerged from the light. A stack of dirty dishes sat in the sink. There was nothing out of the ordinary, though.

She asked, "Is anyone here? Mom? Dad? *Hello?*"

There was no response.

Tiffany hopped and gasped, startled. A flurry of wind caused the windows to rattle and screech. The blinds waved and the curtains swayed, allowing a wave of moonlight to pour into the room.

Tiffany furrowed her brow as she examined the living room, holding her hands over her chest. She stared at the corner between the large flat-screen television and the open window. The curtains swayed near the corner and she could see a silhouette in the darkness—*a human figure.* The first thought in her mind: *a home invasion, just like the movies.*

As she stepped into the living room, Tiffany stuttered, "Wh–Who... Who are you?" Again, there was no response. As her breathing intensified, she said, "I called the cops already. My friends can hear everything, too. They can–"

Mid-sentence, she ran forward and approached an end-table beside the couch. She turned the knob on a lamp and illuminated the living room. Wide-eyed, she quickly turned her attention to the corner. To her utter surprise, the silhouette vanished. She stared at the corner with a deadpan expression, then she burst into a nervous chuckle of relief.

She whispered, "Oh, shit... It was all in my head. It was all in my damn head. I've been watching too many horror movies..."

She closed the window and turned off the light, then she entered the kitchen. She opened the refrigerator and examined her options—water, milk, orange juice, or soda. She took a swig of orange juice from the carton. She was thirsty, but she was also trying to buy some time. She genuinely feared the silhouette in the living room and she didn't want to appear frightened in front of her friends.

She closed her eyes and sighed, mentally preparing herself for the verbal onslaught. *They're just words,* she thought, *these assholes are my friends.*

As she walked down the hall, Tiffany shouted, "I'm coming, idiots! Don't worry, I wasn't checking myself out, either!" She walked into her room and said, "I just left the window open and–"

She stopped as she caught a glimpse of her laptop. The video chat changed. Melanie cried as she spoke on her phone, Kyle frantically tapped the screen on his cell phone, and Hailey disconnected from the chat.

"What the fuck?" Tiffany whispered. She sat on her bed and placed the earbuds in her ears. She asked, "What are you guys planning? What–"

Hysterical, Melanie shouted, "Get out of the house! Run!"

"What's going–"

"He's in your closet, Tiffany! *Run!*"

Tiffany froze upon hearing the explanation. She felt as if time had slowed to a crawl. She could feel each bead of sweat slowly trickling down the nape of her neck, she could count each thumping heartbeat in her chest. One-by-one, she pulled the earbuds out of her ears. She glanced over her shoulder and stared at the closet next to the bedroom door.

With a quivering lip, she whispered, "Oh, shit..."

The closet door swung open. A tall, brawny person stood in her closet, his dark clothing contrasting against her colorful wardrobe. The intruder wore a long black raincoat, dark pants, and matching steel-toe boots. The hood of his coat covered his head. A white paper-mâché mask veiled his face.

The mask was expressionless. Red lipstick was smeared on the lips and eye-shadow was applied around the eye holes. Streams of red paint were marked on the cheeks, as if the person were crying tears of blood. The mask was poignant and terrifying. The knife in the intruder's gloved hand, however, was much more horrifying.

Tiffany ran towards the door and shouted, "Help! Somebody help me!"

She yelped as the intruder grabbed a fistful of her hair and pulled her back into the room. She lost her footing and staggered to her knees in front of the bed.

Melanie watched in horror as the intruder violently tugged on her friend's flannel shirt. The shirt stretched and ripped, then the garment fell to the floor. The masked person effortlessly ripped Tiffany's bra from her chest.

As she fell onto her bed, one arm covering her breasts while swinging at the intruder with the other, Tiffany cried, "Don't! Please, *don't!* Don't do this! Don't rape me! Oh, God, don't rape me!"

As she watched the assault from her laptop, eyes

full of tears, Melanie yelled, "Don't touch her! Don't you dare touch her, you sick bastard!"

The intruder was not daunted by the pleas or the strikes. Despite her resistance, he pulled Tiffany's panties off. He grabbed her arm and pulled her off of the bed. He forced her to stand in front of the laptop as she sobbed and babbled—as if he were modeling her tight figure for the webcam. He held his hand over her mouth, then he glided the blade across her stomach.

Tiffany squirmed in his arms, whimpering and trembling, but she couldn't escape his grip. Melanie's eyes widened as the call connected.

A female operator answered, "911, what is the nature of your emergency?"

Melanie shouted, "My friend! He's hurting my friend! You have to help her!"

"Okay. Please calm down, ma'am. Tell me: who's hurting your friend? Where are you?"

"She–She's at 2314 Forest Avenue. You have to help her. Someone is... is attacking her in her room. He's going to–"

She held her hand over her mouth and gasped, shocked. She watched as the masked intruder stabbed Tiffany's stomach. Hoarse gasps seeped from between the person's fingers as the young woman struggled to breathe. Blood spewed from her lower abdomen as the blade viciously penetrated her stomach *eight* times. Her stomach, crotch, and legs were drenched in blood.

As Tiffany fell to her knees, stunned by the violent attack and disoriented due to her loss of blood, the intruder shoved his fingers past her lips and pried her mouth open. He grabbed her tongue with his fingertips and tried to pull it past her lips.

To his dismay, Tiffany chomped down on his fingers with all of her might. The intruder grunted and groaned. He was bothered by Tiffany's resistance, but he wasn't discouraged. Her teeth could grip and pinch his fingers, but she couldn't penetrate his thick gloves.

So, the masked intruder stabbed into Tiffany's chin, thrusting the knife upward *into* her mouth and through her tongue.

Tiffany, shocked by the attack, released his fingers. Her eyelids flickered and her bottom lip quivered. She wheezed and groaned, unable to cope with the pain.

The intruder grabbed a fistful of Tiffany's hair and pulled her head back, then he turned her towards the camera—the knife still jammed in her jaw. The view was perfect. He thrust the knife in-and-out of her chin, sawing through the tendons and ligaments in her jaw—all while tugging on her bottom teeth.

Blood cascaded across her neck and chest, drenching the rest of her body. Droplets of blood dripped from her erect nipples, like milk from a mother's teat. Bubbling, crackling, and crunching sounds echoed through the room as the intruder tore Tiffany's jaw from her head, which left her mutilated tongue dangling over her bloodied neck. Her tongue swung left-and-right like a pendulum, cut in half and barely attached to her mouth.

Due to the loss of blood and sheer shock, Tiffany passed away during the jaw removal. The intruder pushed her aside. He leaned forward and gazed directly at the webcam. His crystal blue eyes sparkled with a glimmer of deviance—zany, malevolent eyes. His face couldn't be seen, but he clearly smiled behind the mask.

He closed the laptop and ended the video chat.

Chapter Two

Breaking News

Charlene Sanchez ran her fingers through her curly black hair as she stared at her reflection on the mirror near the front door. A high school senior, she didn't draw much attention to herself in terms of style. She wore a simple white top, a black skirt, and matching flats. Her lustrous brown eyes and tender smile could hypnotize any man, though. Despite her beauty, she remained kind and humble.

From the kitchen, Janice Sanchez, her mother, yelled, "Charlene! Don't leave without talking to me! I'm serious this time."

Charlene sighed, then she approached the archway. She stared at her mother, her lips puckered. The short, frail woman stood in front of the sink, washing the morning dishes. She didn't have her daughter's youth, but she could match her beauty and kindness.

Janice glanced back at the archway and said, "I want you to be careful today. I don't want you to stay out too late. I know I can't keep you locked up after school, but... I just don't want you out there with this crazy mess going on."

Charlene responded, "I know, I know. I'll be back before nighttime. I promise."

"Good. After what happened to that poor girl... It's just not safe out there right now. I don't know what I'd do if the same thing happened to you. I don't–"

"It's *not* going to happen to me," Charlene interrupted, trying to stop her mother from spiraling into a tailspin of madness. "I knew Anna. She was a good girl, but she got into some trouble a few times. I guess she probably had enemies. You know, *haters?* I'm not like her. I'll be okay, mom."

Janice scratched her eyebrow and nodded, fighting the urge to cry. If she had it her way, she would have locked Charlene in her room until the killer was caught. She trusted her daughter, she respected her privacy, but she didn't feel comfortable in a world full of strangers. Anyone could be the killer.

She waved and said, "Okay. Go on. I don't want you to be late for school." As she turned towards the sink, she shouted, "I love you!"

Charlene tossed her bag over her shoulder and yelled, "Love you, too!"

The teenager walked out of the house, casually strolling across the porch and walkway. She took a left turn past the white picket fence.

As she walked down the sidewalk, her father, Robert Sanchez, parked in front of the house. The rough man wore navy coveralls—his uniform. He had a head of disheveled hair and prickly stubble on his jaw. He nodded and waved at his daughter. He was arriving home after his night shift.

Charlene returned the wave and nod, then she mouthed: "See you soon. Love you."

She continued walking down the suburban street. She couldn't help but smile as she glanced around the neighborhood. The houses and lawns were beautiful, maintained and organized. Children ran up-and-down the street while teenagers casually walked on the sidewalks or waited for their rides. The neighborhood was bathed in warm sunshine. Disregarding the murder looming over the city, the day was perfect.

"Hey!" a soft, feminine voice said from over her shoulder.

Charlene glanced back and smiled.

Britney Cook approached her friend, a textbook clenched in her arms and a bag slung over her shoulder. Like Charlene, she didn't try to draw attention to herself. She wore a white top, tight black leggings, and brown boots. She could control her style, but she couldn't control her figure. She was naturally curvaceous, so she still caught unwanted attention from her male peers.

In fact, even some of her female classmates were caught staring at her.

As the pair walked beside each other, Charlene asked, "How's it going?"

"I'm good," Britney responded with a casual shrug. "My mom was practically *fighting* to keep me home today 'cause of what happened to Anna. She's just too... overbearing, you know?"

"Yeah. My mom was acting the same way. I get it, though. Anna's gone. She's... She's dead. It's so sad. I can't imagine what her parents are going through. I mean, if the rumors are true, just imagine seeing someone you love killed like... *like that.* It's scary stuff."

Britney sighed and nodded, agreeing without uttering a word. She had heard the rumors and she was disheartened by her classmate's unfortunate death. Charlene frowned as she glanced up at the clear blue sky. She wondered if Anna was watching them from the heavens above.

Breaking the ruminative mood, Britney asked, "Anyway, how are you and Adam doing? Is he still acting like a little asshole or what?"

Charlene chuckled and shook her head. *Yes*—the answer was obvious, but she couldn't quite blurt it out. Adam Allen, her high school sweetheart, had grown distant over the past year. She didn't want to add fuel to the fire by insulting him behind his back.

She responded, "It's hard, you know? I love him with all of my heart, I really do, but things have changed. He... He's just not the same. I think it's because we didn't have any classes together this year, so he just started growing distant. He doesn't call me every night, he doesn't even answer his texts... It's going to get worse, too. Did I tell you? We're probably going to different colleges."

"I'm sorry to hear that, hun. I don't know, though. Maybe it's for the better. If it's not meant to be, it's not meant to be. I hope you can fix your issues, though, 'cause you guys make a cute couple."

The pair shared a giggle. Britney was trying to break the tension, Charlene was trying to keep a semblance of control.

As she glanced at each passing house, Britney said, "About college... How are you feeling?"

"Aside from my little problem with Adam? I'm feeling okay, I guess."

"Well, I'm not. I got accepted to a few, but... I'm afraid it'll just be more of the same. I'm a cheerleader, right? I'm good-looking, *right?*"

Charlene furrowed her brow as she laughed. She joked, "You're conceited, right?"

"I'm serious, Charles. I feel like no one takes me seriously because they're too busy staring at my damn tits or my ass. It pisses me off. I work my ass off—not literally, obviously—and I still get treated like some bimbo. It's annoying and I don't want it to be like that in college, too."

"Well, I know you're smart—smart and beautiful. Forget about everyone else. Fuck 'em," Charlene said with a big grin on her face.

Britney returned the smile, elated by her friend's supportive response. She asked, "Have you heard about Michael and Dominique?"

"What about them?"

"They're having some 'relationship' issues, too. I heard Dominique has been cheating and Michael has been getting suspicious. He's asking friends and he's practically stalking her on Facebook like some sort of psycho."

Charlene sighed and shook her head, amused by her friend's interest in gossip. She asked, "And, why are you telling me this?"

Britney shrugged and said, "I don't know. It's convenient, I guess. I just wanted to make you feel like you weren't the only one with relationship issues."

A blaring horn echoed through the street, causing the couple to hop and gasp. They glanced back at the street and chuckled in relief. A black sedan pulled into the side of the road beside them.

Michael Miller sat in the driver's seat, sunglasses veiling his eyes. His hair was slicked back, a lock of hair dangling over his forehead. A varsity baseball player, he wore a letterman jacket with his school's colors. He was effortlessly cool.

Dominique Martinez sat in the passenger seat. The young woman wore her cheerleader uniform with pride. Unlike her friends, she actively sought attention from anyone who was willing to look her way. She was a tease—and a suspected cheater.

The couple beckoned to Charlene and Britney. The girls glanced at each other and giggled.

Britney whispered, "Speak of the devil."

"Hurry up!" Dominique shouted from the car. "Get in here if you want a ride! We don't have all day!"

As the pair ran to the car, Charlene yelled, "We're coming, we're coming!"

Charlene stopped as she reached the side of the car. From the corner of her eye, she caught a glimpse of a peculiar person. She felt compelled to look. She slowly turned and glanced over at the parallel sidewalk, curious.

A person stood at the corner, waiting for the light to change. Due to his clothing, he stood out like a sore thumb. He wore a black raincoat, black jeans, and black boots—black from head-to-toe. The hood of his coat covered his face. It wasn't raining, though. Compared to the teens and children standing at the stop with him, he appeared malicious.

The first thought in Charlene's mind: *a school shooter?* She grimaced and shook her head, disgusted with her preconceived idea. *He's just a normal kid,* she thought, *don't make assumptions like that, Charles.*

From the driver's seat, Michael asked, "Are you

getting in or not?"

Snapping out of her contemplation, Charlene said, "I'm coming, I'm coming."

She glanced back at the corner—the light already changed and the group already crossed the street. She shrugged it off. She climbed into the backseat and sat beside Britney. They said their hellos, then they sped off to school.

***

The wheels howled as the car skidded to a stop in the senior parking lot. The friends hopped out of the car and walked towards the three-story indoor school, casually chatting and bickering. The morning was normal—except for the news van parked in front of the school. A crowd of nosy students surrounded the van and the news crew, recording the commotion with their phones.

Katie Williams, a local news anchor in a beautiful crimson dress, stood near the school's sign. She swiped her fingers across her red-brown hair and adjusted her earpiece as she prepared to record a segment for the local news. She sneered in disgust and waved at the surrounding students, gesturing her demands—*shoo, shoo.*

Of course, the obnoxious students didn't listen to her.

Charlene asked, "What's going on over there?"

Michael responded, "I have no idea." He nodded at the front of the school. He said, "Check it out: the cops are here, too."

As they approached the front of the school, Charlene leaned towards her right and gazed at the news van. Two black-and-white police cruisers were parked behind the van. A police officer sat in one of the cars while the other cruiser was vacant. The other officers were nowhere in sight.

Curious, Charlene asked, "Do you think they caught Anna's killer?"

Dominique smirked and said, "Well, let's ask this stoner over here." As they approached the van, Dominique shouted, "Stephen! My plug! What's going on?"

Stephen Walker glanced over at Dominique and smiled upon spotting the group. Dominique didn't make him smile, though. *My plug*—if their teachers heard her, he would have been searched by campus security and they would have found his stash of marijuana. He only smiled because he saw Charlene. He liked her.

Stephen was younger than the group of friends. He was a junior at the high school, but he found himself with a large group of friends thanks to his drugs. His beach blonde hair was long and tousled. His clothing was clean, but none of it matched. He wore a green short-sleeve shirt over a white long-sleeve shirt, khaki pants, and white sneakers. He didn't care very much about his appearance.

Stephen asked, "What's up? You guys heard about all of this or what?"

Charlene said, "No. We just got here. What happened?"

"Did they catch the killer?" Britney asked.

Stephen chuckled, then he said, "No. I mean, *hell no.* Someone else was killed last night."

"You're kidding?"

"Nope. Someone died last night, man. I guess it's

connected to Anna's death, too. I heard the police are going to be on campus all *fucking* day. Investigating and interrogating, you know? They're going to have counseling and all of that shit, too. I guess we're not smoking here today..."

The group was startled by the revelation, lost in thoughts of violence and death. One murder in a month was already abnormal in the peaceful city. Two brutal murders in less than a week was a horrifying fact to swallow. A serial killer was clearly on the loose.

Breaking the silence, Michael joked, "Maybe it would be best if we all left town until they catch this psycho. Right? Let's go to Vegas or something. Hell, it's only a few hours away. I could even get us some fake IDs."

"I wouldn't do that, man. If a killer doesn't get you here, some gangsters will probably take your kidney over there," Stephen explained, referencing an old urban legend.

"Well, I'd rather lose my kidney than my life. Besides, if you go with us, you might finally lose your virginity. Hell, we can sell our kidneys to pay for a high-class hooker for you."

"Fuck off."

Michael laughed at his own joke, amused by his crass sense of humor. The rest of the group remained quiet. Someone just died, so it wasn't the best time to make jokes about sex. Michael sighed and nodded—*sorry.*

Stephen said, "You know, I heard she was killed like Anna. Her jaw and her tongue were *ripped* off her head. It's... It's crazy, man."

"*She?*" Charlene repeated, baffled. "How do you know he killed a girl? Did they already say who died?"

"No, not yet. But, if we're talking about a serial killer, he's more than likely killing women and children. That's what serial killers do. That's how the world works. It has something to do with the... the *psychology* of a serial killer. That's why you probably won't see any guys die this time around."

Charlene stared down at her feet, dismayed by the response. She didn't bother to argue with Stephen. She figured he spent too much time watching crime documentaries on YouTube while smoking weed. Still, it seemed like a reasonable assumption. *A serial killer targeting high school students,* she thought, *who could be next?*

Charlene coughed to clear her throat, then she asked, "Have you seen Adam, Stephen?"

"Nope. I just smoked with him on Friday, though. He owes me, too, so–"

"I'm not paying you," Charlene interrupted. She flicked her finger across her phone and said, "He hasn't been answering my calls or texts all weekend. Have any of you seen him?"

No, nope, and no—those were the responses she received from her friends. She rolled her eyes and shook her head, then she shoved her phone into her bag. She marched away from the van and headed towards the building.

As his friends walked away, Stephen shouted, "Wait up! Don't you guys want to watch the news! It's live! Like, really live!"

Without looking back, Charlene shook her head

and shouted, "No! She doesn't know shit!"

Michael, Dominique, and Britney rushed to catch up to their friend. They all slowed to a stroll in front of the school's entrance as they spotted their principal, Andrew Lopez. The man adjusted his tie as he scowled at the news van. He was friendly around his students, some would call him a pushover, but he despised the media's exploitative use of tragedy—especially when it involved his students.

Charlene stopped near the principal and asked, "What's happening, Mr. Lopez? Is it true? Did someone else die?"

Lopez's scowl turned into a frown upon hearing the question. He could hear the sincere fear in Charlene's voice. He was responsible for their safety. The coffins of Anna and Tiffany sat on his shoulders, burdening him with guilt.

He said, "We're having an assembly after first period. We'll have an open conversation about everything then. Okay?" A bell rang before any of the students could respond. The principal said, "Go to class. I'm going to get rid of these leeches."

The students watched as the man marched towards the news van, pushing his sleeves up and loosening his tie on the way. They smiled as they watched their principal throwing a fit in front of the camera and ruining Katie's shot.

Charlene sighed, then she said, "I guess we'll have to wait to find out what happened. Let's just go to class."

"Yeah, come on," Britney said.

The students strolled down the hallway and headed to their classrooms before the tardy bell could ring.

Chapter Three

First Period

Charlene blankly stared at the whiteboard from the back of the classroom. Numbers and letters were scrawled on the board in black marker, but the equations were blurred in her eyes. The numbers drifted closer to each other, overlapping to create an image of muddled nonsense. Due to her overwhelming stress, mathematics was nothing but a foreign language to the young woman.

With listless eyes, she stared at her teacher—*Mr. Collin Wilson.*

Wilson was young, charismatic, and handsome. His feathery brown hair was tousled, his prickly stubble was trimmed. The sleeves on his button-up shirt were rolled up to his elbows, revealing his firm, vascular forearms. He was clearly strong. His style was plain—a button-up shirt, brown trousers, and matching dress shoes—but he was still attractive.

Yet, amidst the murder and mayhem, Wilson couldn't capture the attention of his class. His attractive features could not woo the young women, his suave personality could not attract the susceptible young men.

Charlene glanced over at a group of senior girls to her left. She could hear their whispers as they childishly gossiped. Smiles were plastered on their faces and laughter escaped their mouths as they discussed the rumored murder from the previous night.

A blonde-haired teenager smirked and whispered, "I heard Melanie isn't here because she saw it. She saw her die and she's all 'traumatized' and shit. She's such a little bitch. She acts like no one has ever died before. I mean, people die in movies all the time, right?"

In a soft tone, just above a whisper, her friend responded, "That's what I'm saying. She's such a drama queen. She's always been like that."

Charlene furrowed her brow as she eavesdropped on the conversation. She didn't care about their stupidity—people dying in movies wasn't the same as people dying in real life. She was only concerned about her classmate. She leaned forward in her seat and stared at a vacant desk towards the front of the class—Melanie's seat.

She found a piece of the puzzle, flooding her mind with hundreds of theories. *Melanie witnessed the murder,* she thought, *she'll know something about it.* She turned back in her seat and stared at Britney, who sat directly behind her. Britney returned the stare. The pair shared the same thought: *we have to find out more.*

Gossip and rumors were unreliable, harmful, and toxic—but the couple *absolutely* needed to know more.

Charlene leaned closer to the blonde and asked, "Are you guys talking about Anna or the... the 'new' one?"

"We're talking about Tiff. You know, Tiffany Anderson? She's that slutty girl who sits in the front of the class. I heard she got, you know, *whacked* last night or whatever they say. They even said it was uploaded online. Maybe even on Facebook. I'm not going to look it up, though."

"Tiffany..." Charlene repeated in disbelief.

She stared down at her lap as she brooded over the news. The rumored tragedy broke her heart. They weren't the closest friends, but she knew Tiffany since middle school. Her eyes darted left-and-right as she glanced around the room. She stared at another empty desk near the front of the class—Tiffany's seat. *It's true,* she thought, *it's all true.*

The blonde continued, "Anyway, we were just saying: Melanie supposedly saw everything. She's at home because she's 'traumatized' about it. She's scared, I guess."

"*Scared?*" Britney repeated in an uncertain tone.

"Yeah, scared. If it's true, Tiffany's killer saw Melanie's face. Plus, the killer supposedly stole Tiffany's laptop and cell phone. That psycho definitely knows where she lives. Shit, he might have *everyone's* information by now."

Britney clarified, "Everyone who talked to her. If your number's not in her phone, then you're safe, right? I mean, I barely knew her." She glanced over at Charlene and asked, "What about you?"

Charlene did not respond. Her phone number was on Tiffany's phone—that fact was irrefutable. She wondered if the killer had access to her home address, too. Her mind was addled as she tried to remember every message she ever sent to Tiffany. *Did I send her my address? Is my address on the internet? Can he find me?*—the questions ran through her mind.

"I need you to be quiet back there," Wilson said as he tapped the board with his marker. "I know there's a lot going on today, but this is also important. It's going to be on the next test and I won't be grading on a curve. You know that. So, pay attention. Thank you."

Wilson turned his back on the class and continued to scribble on the board. He babbled about the equations, but his students weren't listening.

Unable to keep her mouth shut, Britney asked, "What happened, Wilson?"

The teacher glanced back with a furrowed brow. He asked, "What are you talking about?"

"What's happening out there? There are all these rumors going around, but no one is telling us the truth. There was a news van outside this morning. There are police outside *and* inside our school. And, we're going to have an 'emergency' assembly. What's this all about? Did something really happen? Are we safe?"

Wilson placed his hands on his hips and sighed. It wasn't his role to discuss the crime with the students, it wasn't his job to inform them of the lurking dangers. He frowned and nodded as his students began to chatter. He could hear them talking about their safety while referencing the rumors: *am I next? Is the killer in our school?*

The teacher tapped his marker on the white board, as if the writing utensil were a judge's gavel. He called for silence.

"Quiet down, quiet down," Wilson said, irked. As

the student chatter dwindled, he explained, "There was an incident last night. You will be told everything you need to know at the assembly. Okay? Principal Lopez will give you as much information as possible. I know there will be counseling available throughout the week, too, so you don't have to worry about anything."

"There wouldn't be any counseling if it wasn't serious," Britney remarked, adding fuel to the fire.

Again, Wilson sighed and lowered his head. He couldn't control his students. Rumors were prone to the snowball effect. Unfortunately, rumors were also part of the high school social life. And, the high school social life was comprised of susceptible teenagers who would believe anything.

Over the gossip, Wilson said, "Everything is under control. Even if it was serious, we're going to take care of you. Don't let fear take control of your lives like this. Don't let rumors interfere with your education. We have–"

The bell disrupted his speech. As if the bell had broken a trance, the concern in the room vanished. The students grabbed their bags and stood from their seats, ready to continue the monotonous day.

Wilson shouted, "All seniors are going to the gym! Tell your friends if they don't know!"

Chapter Four

The Assembly

"Cheer up, Charles," Britney said as she gently pushed Charlene. She said, "We're going to get more 'juicy' details at this assembly. It won't be much, but it should make you feel better, right? Come on, give me a smile."

Charlene kept her head down as she walked down the hall with her friend. She contemplated the rumors, thinking about all of the possible outcomes. Britney's optimistic outlook could not whisk away her negative thoughts. An assembly couldn't take her contact information out of Tiffany's phone. She needed a bigger distraction—and it was right around the corner.

Charlene and Britney hopped and gasped as they clashed with Adam Allen in the hallway. Britney fell to her knees to pick up her textbook and worksheets, muttering about the young man's negligence—*watch where you're going, idiot.* Charlene stepped in reverse and stared at Adam, shocked by his sudden appearance.

Adam cracked a smile as he stared back at her. He wasn't like Michael or Stephen. He wasn't a jock or a dealer—he was somewhere in between. He was a fit and handsome young man with wavy black hair who happened to enjoy recreational drugs. His style was simple, too. He wore an opened button-up shirt with a white t-shirt underneath, blue jeans, and sneakers.

Like his girlfriend, Charlene, he didn't draw attention to himself. He liked to fly under the radar to avoid drama and trouble.

Adam asked, "Where are you guys going? Aren't your classes the other way?"

As she marched forward, Charlene responded, "We have an assembly today."

Britney shoved Adam with a swing of her hips, then she followed her friend. She said, "We have to go to the gym. Come on, asshole." She glanced back at Adam and said, "You have a lot of catching up to do if you haven't heard all of the rumors."

Adam sighed in disappointment, then he jogged to catch up to the girls. He asked, "Charlene, are you mad at me?"

"Why are you late today?" Charlene asked without slowing her pace.

"Why was I late? I slept in. Is there a problem with that?"

"Why haven't you been answering my calls or texts?"

Adam chuckled, then he said, "I don't have service right now, Charles. I can't call you or answer *hundreds* of your text messages if I don't have service."

Charlene asked, "Why don't you have service? Hmm?"

Adam furrowed his brow and shook his head, baffled by the questions. He slowed down and carefully analyzed his girlfriend's passive-aggressive demeanor. The couple hit a rough patch in their relationship, but Charlene was unusually hostile. He felt as if he were being interrogated by a cop who was out of leads and frustrated.

Adam pulled on Charlene's shoulder, stopping her from moving forward. He asked, "What's up with you? Did someone die or something?" He chuckled and shrugged, then he said, "I mean, someone other than Anna."

Her lip curling in disgust, Charlene responded, "Yeah, someone else died, Adam. Tiffany was killed last night."

Chiming in, Britney said, "And they said she died the same way Anna did."

Adam gazed into Charlene's glistening eyes, then he glanced over at Britney. He waited for the punchline to a joke, but the young women remained quiet and serious.

Adam nodded and said, "Shit. I saw the cops outside before I got here. I thought I missed a fight or something. That's... That's too bad."

"Yeah. Let's just go to the gym before they lock us out," Charlene said.

The group continued walking down the hall, dodging the freshman running to class and waving at the juniors who would miss the assembly. Stephen, for example, nodded and waved at the group as he strolled into his video production class. Arms around each other, Michael and Dominique joined the group. Michael and Adam shook hands while Dominique waved at Charlene and Britney.

Adam asked, "You think Stephen is holding right now? I wanna smoke during lunch if he's down."

Dominique rolled her eyes and said, "Someone just died, man."

"I know, but it's not like I knew her. I think I had

her for one class in the last four years. Besides, you remember the dead better when you're high. Weed makes everything better, so, you know, it'll help me remember Tiffany. I know it."

Charlene said, "She just died last night and you're acting like she died years ago. If you can't remember her from last week, then maybe weed is the problem."

The group walked into the gym. They squeezed past their classmates and sat at the top of the bleachers.

***

From the top of the bleachers, Charlene examined the gym. Senior students filled the benches—some gossiped about the rumors, others spoke about their dull lives. The seniors sat in cliché cliques, including the jocks, the cheerleaders, the freaks, and the geeks. She was bothered by the selfish cliques, worried about the inevitable outcasts.

Yet, she found some relief in knowing she would be escaping the toxic high school environment soon. Graduation was right around the corner and most of the cliques would crumble in the college environment—fraternities and sororities were a different story. She turned her attention to the center of the gym.

The center circle of the basketball court was turned into a makeshift stage. Two microphone stands sat in the circle while two cameras were aimed at the stage. The cameras live-streamed the assembly to the classes that could not attend. The vice principal and a few counselors sat near the makeshift stage, sweat spurting from their glands like water from a sprinkler.

Principal Andrew Lopez and Sheriff Cameron Jackson entered the center circle. Jackson grabbed a microphone. He coughed and grunted to clear his throat, preparing himself for a difficult speech.

He paced back-and-forth on the stage and said, "Listen up, ladies and gentlemen. We've been here before. I understand this school is still reeling from the tragic loss of a classmate, Anna Lee. We told you everything we could about that case. Rest assured, we are still investigating her death. I also understand that there have been some rumors circulating over the past twelve hours. Well, let's set a few things straight."

He lowered the microphone down to his chest as he examined the quiet audience. The students looked to him for reassurance. Unfortunately, he couldn't offer them the guaranteed security they sought.

He said, "Last night, Tiffany Anderson passed away. Some of you may have known her, some of you may have never heard of her. The fact remains: a classmate, *a young girl,* passed away. Furthermore, we're fairly certain she was murdered. Was it the same suspect from Anna's murder? Do we know who is committing these disgusting crimes? Well, I can't answer all of your questions at this assembly. I can't and I won't. We don't want to frighten you and we don't want to encourage any copycat crimes. We *will* have a talk with your parents, though. We'll be contacting all of your parents and guardians throughout the day so they can come speak to me this afternoon at a conference here at school. Your parents will take care of everything. You have my word on that. That's all I have for you now, unfortunately."

Jackson clenched his jaw and shook his head as the audience bickered and booed. He didn't shout for silence, though. He allowed them to vent for a moment. He felt responsible for the death in the city after all.

As the shouting dwindled to a few whispers, Jackson said, "Thank you for your patience, ladies and gentlemen. Principal Lopez has a few words for you now."

Lopez grabbed the other microphone and said, "I never thought I'd have to talk to you about something like this *two* times in one week. It's hard for me, so I can only imagine how hard it is for you. I know it's scary out there these days. With all your other problems, it's probably really hard to get out of bed in the morning. But, you *have* to get up. You have to go out into the world and live your lives. You have to be safe and vigilant, but you can't let something like this control your lives. I want you to remember that. You're strong and we're here to help you find your strength if you can't find it on your own."

He lowered the microphone and watched his students with glistening eyes. The students were not perfect, but he was proud of them. He vowed to protect and help them during high school and beyond. He could see his speech was working, too. The students were still frightened, but he could see the determination in their eyes.

Lopez continued, "There's a lot we can talk about.

I know how tragedy can affect people, especially young adults like yourselves. Believe me, I've been there before. I just want you to know that your feelings are normal and you can talk to us about anything. Counseling will be available before, during, and after school for the rest of the week. We're giving you our full support, okay? *Okay?*"

Unsynchronized, the students said: *Yeah, okay, great.*

Lopez nodded and said, "Good, good. Thank you for your patience and understanding. That goes for all you seniors and everyone else at our great school. We're here for you. Now, go to your second period and please resume your day as–"

"*Wait!*" Charlene shouted as she stood from her seat. She grimaced as the students and faculty turned towards her. Teary-eyed, she said, "You can't just end it like... like *that.* We can't wait until nighttime to find out what's going on from our parents. Just tell us: did he really steal Tiffany's phone? Does he have our numbers? Our addresses?"

Jackson and Lopez glanced at each other, disappointed. The look in their eyes said: *shit.*

Jackson said, "I'm advising everyone in this school to avoid the rumors. Don't talk about 'em, don't spread 'em."

"Please, just answer the questions. Did he steal Tiffany's phone? Does he have our information?"

"Nothing is certain right now. A phone and a laptop were stolen from the crime scene. *However,* we recovered the stolen property this morning. We're trying to find out if the suspect extracted any information from the devices. Like I said, nothing is certain."

"So, how do we know if we're safe?" Britney asked.

Jackson responded, "We've taken steps to ensure your safety. For the next few weeks, or until the suspect is captured, we will be actively watching the school. We will monitor all of your school events. And, we will be patrolling your neighborhoods more frequently. No one is going to get hurt. You have my word."

Lopez said, "If you have any other questions, you can talk to any faculty member between classes, during lunch, and after school. Please, try to resume your day normally. Your teachers are waiting to continue your second period classes. Thank you for your time."

Charlene did not move. The seniors, including her friends, walked away from the bleachers as if nothing were wrong. The young woman was tormented by the mystery, though. She needed answers to her questions—and she planned on finding them.

Chapter Five

Lunch and Gossip

Lunch was available in the cafeteria for all students. Seniors and juniors were allowed to leave campus for lunch, though. Several small restaurants and convenience stores surrounded the school, vying for the students' lunch money. The group of friends found themselves outside of a local burger place—*Big's Burgers.*

Charlene, Britney, Dominique, and Michael sat at a table, shielded from the sun by a large umbrella. Adam and Stephen stood around the corner of the building, smoking weed in the shadows.

As she absently stared at the neighboring intersection, counting the passing cars, Charlene said, "I just can't believe this is happening. Anna just died last week. Tiffany died last night... Anyone could be next, right?"

Dominique tossed a French fry into her mouth, then she said, "Don't think like that, Charles. As far as we know, Anna and Tiffany just got in with the wrong crowd. Both of them had big, *nasty* mouths. All of this... It could all blow over by the end of the week."

"She's right," Britney added. She took a sip of her soda, then she said, "They didn't say it was a serial killer or anything like that. We're just making that assumption. You know what they say about assumptions. They make you look like an ass... or something like that."

Charlene sighed in disappointment. She was bothered by her friends' negligence. Michael was too busy fiddling with his phone to even participate in the conversation. She didn't expect Stephen or Adam to add any helpful input, either. She leaned back in her seat and glanced back at the pass-through window on the restaurant.

A group of junior girls ordered their food while gossiping about Tiffany's murder. They appeared to know more about Tiffany's death. Like cancer cells, the rumors were growing. She recognized a red-haired girl in the group—*Melody.*

Charlene wasn't the type to gossip or eavesdrop, but her curiosity got the best of her. She scooted back in her seat and listened to the group. Britney, knowing her friend well, smiled and scooted closer to the girls, too. She wasn't worried about her safety like Charlene, but she was curious. *Who didn't want to hear about the dead?*

Melody said, "I heard Kyle and Hailey also saw her die."

A brunette girl responded, "Kyle? Kyle Webb?"

"Yeah. Melanie, Kyle, Hailey, and Tiffany were having a Skype chat or something like that. They saw her die. When the cops find out, there's going to be a *big* scene. I bet you Kyle's going to try to run. He always does."

Interrupting the conversation, Charlene asked, "Is that true?"

Melody held her hand over her chest and hopped, startled by Charlene's soft voice. She nervously smiled upon spotting Charlene.

She said, "Hey, Charles. You scared me. Were... Were you just listening to us?"

"You're talking out loud right next to us and in front of a cashier. Does it really matter? Was all of that true? About Kyle and all of them?"

"Yeah... Well, that's what I heard. I'm not making it up or anything like that."

Charlene turned in her seat and asked, "Who did you hear it from? Huh? How do you know all of this?"

Melody sighed, then she explained, "One of my friends is dating Kyle. He told her everything and she told me. Listen, if she didn't want anyone to know, she shouldn't be telling people. I'm not starting any rumors, I'm just talking about what I heard."

Just talking about what I heard—in other words, she was gossiping and spreading rumors.

Charlene asked, "You said it was *Kyle Webb,* right?" Melody nodded—*yep.* Charlene said, "Okay, thanks. And, don't worry: I won't tell anyone about your gossiping. I don't really care about any of that. See you around."

As Charlene turned in her seat, Britney asked, "Why do you care so much about this? It's tragic and all, but it's really none of our business. Just let the teachers and police handle it."

Charlene sucked her lips inward as if she were trying to stop herself from laughing. She frowned instead. She tried her best to avoid the rumors, she wanted to bury her pessimistic thoughts, but she couldn't escape the truth.

She said, "I'm worried. Tiffany didn't hang out with us, but I had a few classes with her over the years. She had my number and I had hers. We spoke on Facebook, Instagram... *everything.* She had my contact information and I'm worried about that. Aren't you? Whoever killed her could have your home address." She turned to her right and said, "Or even yours, Dom. We could be next."

The group remained silent, unperturbed by the ominous suggestion. Dominique munched on her fries while Michael tapped his phone and shook his head. The sound of a lighter *clicking* emerged as Stephen and Adam smoked a bowl around the corner. Britney stared at Charlene, her lips puckered. She could see the fear in her friend's eyes.

Britney said, "I didn't know her like you did. I don't even think I had her as a friend on Facebook. I'm sorry."

Still chewing her fries, Dominique held her hand over her mouth and said, "I didn't know her, either." She giggled, then she said, "Maybe I need to smoke to remember her better."

Charlene glanced at Michael and asked, "What about you? Do you care at all or are you just going to keep messing with your phone?"

"I didn't know her, Charles," Michael said without taking his eyes off of his phone.

Charlene turned in her seat and stared at the stoners. Eyes welling with tears, she pouted as she gazed at her boyfriend. She begged for a supporting hand without uttering a word. Lungs full of smoke, Adam stared back at her with bloodshot eyes. Smoke billowed from his mouth as he coughed and grunted —the bud was good.

Adam shook his head and said, "Don't look at me.

I didn't know her."

"Shit," Charlene muttered, disappointed. "It's always the same with you..."

"I knew her," Stephen said as he held his breath. He handed the pipe to Adam and exhaled, covering his face with smoke. He said, "She had my number. She knows a lot of my usual 'spots,' too. I sold to her every once in a while."

Charlene asked, "Will you help me?"

"With what?"

"Let's go talk to Kyle. Let's get to the bottom of this."

Stephen clenched his jaw as he considered the request. He already knew the answer—a resounding 'yes'—but he wanted to play it cool.

He said, "Okay, sure. He should be in the cafeteria right now. That's where he usually eats."

As Charlene stood from her seat, Michael said, "We have Kyle in fifth period, Charles. Just talk to him then."

Charlene grabbed Stephen's wrist and pulled him away from the group. As the couple departed, she shouted, "I can't! I have to know what he saw!"

***

"There he is," Stephen said as he nodded at the other end of the cafeteria.

Beyond the bench-tables, Kyle stood with a group of friends near a trash can. All smiles and chuckles, he acted as if nothing were wrong. No one would have suspected him of knowing any significant details about Tiffany's death. He was naturally casual.

Charlene walked ahead, ignoring her other

friends and pushing past her classmates. She marched forward, hurling herself deeper into the mystery. Stephen followed closely behind. He wasn't as serious due to the influence of the marijuana, but he refused to abandon her.

Without uttering a word, Charlene grabbed Kyle's arm and pulled him away from his friends. Kyle nervously smiled and indistinctly mumbled as his friends laughed at him, amused by the situation. He was dragged to a quiet corner in the cafeteria.

Kyle pulled away from Charlene's grip and asked, "What the hell are you doing?" He glanced over at Stephen and asked, "What? Do I owe you money or something? Did you bring your bitch to come beat me up?"

"Fuck off, man," Stephen responded, irked by his insult.

Charlene said, "This isn't about weed. This is about Tiffany—*Tiffany Anderson.* I heard you were there when... when she died. What happened to her?"

Kyle's smile was wiped from his face. He stared at Charlene, then he glanced at Stephen, then he glanced back at Charlene. The expression on his face read: *is she serious?* He thought about running, slipping and sliding past the couple, but he didn't want to cause a scene.

Stony-faced, he said, "I don't know what you're talking about."

"Don't do this the hard way, Kyle. I'm not trying to get you into any trouble. I just need to know the truth. Talk to me. *Please.*"

"I told you: I don't know what you're talking

about. Go smoke some weed and leave me alone."

As Kyle tried to push past her, Charlene said, "If you don't talk to me, I'll tell Sheriff Jackson that you know something." Kyle stopped and glared at her. Charlene nodded and said, "That's right. Call me a 'snitch' or a 'bitch,' but I *will* get to the bottom of this. What happened last night?"

Kyle clenched his jaw and glanced around the cafeteria, as if he were considering his options. His classmates appeared normal, oblivious and happy. They didn't notice the storm of doubt and fear brewing in his mind.

Kyle said, "I really don't know anything. We were talking on Skype. It was... It was Melanie, Hailey, Tiffany, and me. Tiffany heard something in the house, so she left for a few minutes—and she left her laptop open. While she was gone, some guy walked into her room and hid in her closet. He waited for her..."

Stephen asked, "Then he... he killed her?"

"I guess."

"What do you mean you 'guess?' What did you see?" Charlene asked.

Kyle explained, "I didn't see her die. I logged off as soon as he got out of the closet. Like I said, I didn't actually see anything. I didn't see what Melanie *supposedly* saw. I wasn't there."

Charlene nodded as she absorbed the information. *Melanie saw the entire death,* she thought, *I have to talk to her if I want to find the killer.* She stared at Kyle and examined his behavior. His eyes darted left and right as he rubbed the nape of his neck. Sweat glistened on his brow and his breathing was erratic. She could read him like a book—he had more information.

Charlene said, "You said you saw him go into the closet. Did you recognize the killer?"

"First of all, I didn't say that a *guy* was the killer. So, don't go around telling people that I know who did it. I don't want to get involved."

Charlene repeated, "Did you recognize the killer?"

Kyle sighed, then he said, "No. The person I saw was wearing a black raincoat and a mask. It was a white mask with some paint on it. He was bigger than Tiffany, but everyone is... *was* bigger than her. She was a small girl. Maybe he was a guy, maybe he wasn't..."

Charlene furrowed her brow and lowered her head. She stared down at her feet as she thought about the person she saw in the morning. *Black raincoat,* she thought, *is the killer a student?* She shook her head, shrugging off the possibility. She didn't see the person's face after all. He could have been an adult as far as she knew.

"What did the mask look like?" Stephen asked. "Was it the mask from *Scream?* The movie or the TV series? Or was it a knock-off?"

Kyle huffed and shook his head—*this asshole.* He said, "I don't know. I didn't get a good look at it. It was a white mask with a blank expression. There was some paint on his lips and cheeks and... I don't know, okay? It just looked like a weird mask." He squeezed past the pair, then he stopped. He glanced back at Charlene and said, "You shouldn't be worrying about any of this anyway. You're over here acting like a cop with a stoner partner. It'll be better for everyone if you just ignored it. I mean, look around you: everyone is ignoring it. There shouldn't be any problems as long as you don't interfere, okay?"

Charlene responded, "Did you know he took Tiffany's phone and laptop? He could have all of our information. Walking around here pretending like there aren't targets on our backs won't help any of us."

As he walked away, Kyle shrugged and said, "You can't see an invisible target, Charlene. You know what they say about making assumptions."

Infuriated, Charlene watched as Kyle returned to his group of friends. She couldn't help but feel like he was hiding something. She refused to cause a scene, though. If there was a target on her back, she didn't want to make herself visible to the hunter.

Charlene and Stephen glanced at each other—doubtful, worried, *frightened.* Before they could utter a word, the bell rang and called them to their next class.

Chapter Six

Fifth Period

The desks in the classroom were pushed together, forming four small clusters of students. The groups were supposed to discuss the assigned chapter of a novel, presenting their opinions and analyses. Most of the students discussed the rumors of murder instead. The teacher, a haughty middle-aged woman, walked around the groups and examined their interactions.

Charlene sat in a group towards the back of the classroom. Michael sat in the neighboring group. Kyle sat in Michael's group, too. The era of passing notes was long gone. Instead, the students communicated by using their cell phones under their desks and behind their books. Holding her phone under the desk and above her lap, Charlene sent a text message to Michael.

The message read: *Talk to Kyle!!*

She gazed at Michael from across the room, trying to convince him with a set of puppy eyes. To her utter disappointment, the young man didn't glance her way. He furrowed his brow as he checked his phone, as if he had just received a cryptic message. Holding his phone behind his backpack, which sat at the edge of his desk, he quickly composed a message.

Charlene's phone vibrated. She checked her phone and frowned.

Michael's message read: *About what?*

Charlene responded: *About Tiffany!! He knows something. Please talk to him. Please, please, please!!*

Michael did not immediately respond. He took his time to answer his other messages. Charlene grimaced and bounced in her seat, blatantly anxious. Her phone buzzed again.

Michael's message read: *No.*

"Asshole," Charlene muttered.

She glanced at her group. A young brunette girl spoke about the assignment, discussing the underlying themes of the book. She could see her lips moving, but she couldn't hear the girl's words. Charlene was a good student, but her sinister thoughts stopped her from thinking clearly. She puckered her lips and stared down at her cell phone.

She opened a text message thread she shared with Adam. Her last message read: *Why are you always like this? You're always running... I hate it.* The text was followed by a sad emoji. She typed a letter, preparing to send an apology, then she stopped herself. *He doesn't have service,* she thought, *it's useless.*

Instead, she sent another message to Michael: *Has Adam said anything about me? About our status?*

With a creased brow, Charlene glanced over at the neighboring group as Michael laughed. Michael glanced back at Charlene and shrugged, a sly smirk on his face.

He responded to her message: *What would he tell me about you?*

Charlene sighed and dug her fingers into her hair. She was irked by Michael's nonchalant attitude. The pair were friends since middle school, but the baseball player was always distant. He didn't enjoy prying into other people's business because he didn't want the same to happen to him. He had his own relationship issues to handle.

Wide-eyed, Charlene watched as Kyle stood from his seat. The young man approached the teacher at the front of the classroom. His lips flapped, but his voice couldn't be heard over the classroom chatter. Their teacher nodded and spoke, too, but she didn't seem annoyed or angered.

Charlene's mind was flooded with dozens of questions: *what is he up to? Is he going to confess? Is he trying to get away?* She knew he had a knack for fighting and running. She glanced over at Michael with a set of worried eyes.

Michael stared back at her and shrugged—*I don't know a thing.* Kyle smiled and nodded at the teacher. He grabbed a narrow piece of wood from the whiteboard—the bathroom pass—then he casually strolled out of the classroom.

The pieces were easy to link: he was going to the restroom. Yet, due to the violent deaths in the past week, suspicion still reigned supreme.

Charlene snapped out of her contemplation as her phone buzzed. She received a message from Michael.

The message read: *Check the time.*

Charlene tilted her head, baffled. She checked the clock on her phone. It was 1:15 PM. Her phone buzzed again as she received another message from Michael.

The message read: *He ALWAYS goes to the*

bathroom right now. His fucking bladder is on the clock. It's nothing.

Michael easily dismissed the rumors. He didn't think much of Kyle's behavior, either. Everything seemed normal to him. Charlene was a different story. She feared for her safety. Despite the lack of proof, she believed she was being targeted. As a matter of fact, she believed *everyone* at the school was a potential target and she was certain the killer would strike again.

Her classmate asked, "Did you finish the homework, Charlene? Or should we skip you?"

Still lost in her thoughts, Charlene said, "No, no... I finished it. Let me just get my worksheet out."

"Okay."

Charlene couldn't smother her suspicious thoughts, but she tried her best to bury them. She pulled her worksheet out of her bag and finally participated in the group assignment.

***

Kyle rubbed his face with lukewarm water, sniffling and muttering. He was discreet about his knowledge concerning Tiffany's death. He was able to keep his poker face afloat around his peers and teachers. He was cracking under pressure, though. He knew Charlene was snooping and gossiping, he knew the law was breathing down his neck.

He turned off the faucet, then he leaned forward with his palms on the countertop. He stared at his reflection on the mirror. Except for him, the narrow restroom was empty. So, he only saw *his* reflection— and he hated it. He saw a coward and a fool. He bit off more than he could chew and he was struggling to swallow the hard facts.

Kyle whispered, "I pushed myself into a corner, didn't I? Fuck... I should just tell 'em what I saw. If I don't, Charlene will say something and I'll be deeper in this shit. I... I have to tell someone. I have to do something. I fucked up."

He pulled his cell phone out of his pocket. He thought about calling the police to give an anonymous tip. He opened his phone app and dialed 911. He didn't tap the green 'call' prompt, though. He hesitated for a moment, reconsidering all of his options. *I can run away,* he thought, *I can just lay low until they catch the guy.*

A snickering sound emerged from one of the stalls.

Kyle quickly turned and glanced around the bathroom. There were five urinals to his left at the very end of the restroom. Parallel from the sinks, there were five stalls. The entrance waited to his right. He checked under the stalls when he first entered the restroom. It was supposed to be empty. Yet, the snickering sound emerged from the last stall to his left again.

Kyle asked, "Is someone there?" There was no response. He said, "If you're watching me, eavesdropping like some nosy bitch, I swear I'm going to fuck you up. You hear me? Huh? Are you listening to me, asshole?"

Yet again, no one answered.

Kyle swallowed the lump in his throat—*gulp.* He crept forward, walking with wide, careful strides. He approached the last stall. He pulled a pen out of his pocket and popped the cap off. He was ready to stab the eavesdropper. As he touched the stall door, another snickering sound emerged from the last stall to the right. A *thud* quickly followed, as if someone had bumped into the stall wall.

Kyle nervously smiled and asked, "Is this some sort of game? Huh? What are you trying to do to me? What's the point of this?" He kept his eyes low and stared at the gaps under the doors as he approached the other stall. With a devious grin, he asked, "Or, am I walking in on something? Are you fucking in there, hmm? Guy-and-girl or guy-and-guy? Are some fags getting some action in there?"

He couldn't help but chuckle at his offensive remarks. He used his vulgar mouth as a defense mechanism—he was still an asshole, though. He tightly gripped his pen, then he kicked the stall door open. The door wobbled as it hit the wall.

To his utter surprise, the stall was empty. He walked in and examined the stall. The walls, the floor, and the toilet were clean—*spotless,* in fact. He didn't notice any dents on the walls, either. There was nothing out of the ordinary.

As he stared up at the ceiling, Kyle muttered, "What the fuck, man? What the hell is going on here? Am I... Holy shit, am I going crazy?"

Unbeknownst to Kyle, a person's arm protruded from under the stall wall. The person in the neighboring stall held a sharp pocket knife in his gloved hand. His forearm was covered with the sleeve of his black raincoat. As the student mumbled, the hidden person grabbed Kyle's shin with his free hand and sliced Kyle's ankle with the knife.

Kyle didn't have the opportunity to respond or pull away. He shrieked and staggered as blood gushed from his mutilated ankle. The person in the neighboring stall, refusing to release Kyle's shin, cut his ankle again. He sawed into Kyle's Achilles tendon with the sharp blade. Blood dripped onto his leather gloves and spilled onto the floor, but it didn't stop him.

Out of breath, Kyle shouted, "Stop! Stop! Oh, fuck! *Stop it!*"

He fell to his knees and leaned over the toilet, as if he had just spent a night drinking. Tears plunged into the toilet water as he sobbed and babbled. He couldn't form a comprehensible sentence, though. He just screamed at the top of his lungs, hoping someone would hear him. He glanced down at his mangled ankle and grimaced.

His skin, sock, and shoe were drenched in blood, but he could still see the *deep,* peeling gashes on his ankle. Through the blood and flesh, he could see something *white* in the cuts. *Bones?*–he thought. The killer sawed down to the center of his ankle, causing his foot to dangle—barely connected to his leg through a flimsy piece of flesh. His foot was nearly *severed* by the knife.

Teeth chattering, he stuttered, "I–I can't... I can't move my toes. Oh, shit... What... What the fuck did you do?!"

His eyes widened as his attacker stood in front of the stall. He recognized his black raincoat—*Tiffany's killer.*

The killer's mask was different, though. He wore a white paper-mâché plague doctor mask. The eyes were surrounded with eye-shadow. There were streams of red paints under the mask's eyes—trails of bloody tears. Newspaper articles appeared to be purposely wrapped around the beak. The headlines were illegible, but an image of the school was blatant.

The masked killer still held the bloody knife in his right hand. He held a cell phone in his other hand. He aimed the camera at Kyle, as if he were recording him.

Eyes welling with tears, Kyle stuttered, "Wh–Who... Who the hell are you?" As the masked person took one step forward, Kyle shouted, "Help! Help me! Please, someone–"

The killer thrust his knife into Kyle's neck, immediately muffling his screams. He tried to twist the knife, causing the wound to widen. The blade was jammed in his thick flesh, though. It was difficult to cut through the muscle and cartilage—it wasn't like the movies. That didn't stop the masked killer from trying, though.

Wide-eyed, Kyle grabbed the killer's wrist and stared at his attacker in disbelief. A *squelching* sound, bubbling and crackling, emerged from his neck as blood leaked from the wound. He grunted and groaned, but to no avail—he could hardly breathe. Blood spewed from his neck like oil from a blowout as the killer pulled the knife out.

Kyle tightly gripped his neck. It looked as if he were trying to strangle himself. He tried to stop the excessive bleeding, but the blood just spilled from the slits between his fingers. His t-shirt and chest were drenched in blood, too. He glanced every which way, searching for an exit, but the vicious killer cornered him.

His eyes stopped upon spotting the gap under the neighboring stall. *Crawl away,* he thought, *I have to get out of here.* He slipped on the puddle of blood on the floor as he tried to crawl into the neighboring stall.

Before he could escape, the masked person grabbed a fistful of Kyle's wavy hair. He dragged him back into the stall and pulled him closer to the toilet. He dunked his head into the toilet, causing Kyle to kick and squirm as he slowly drowned. His blood quickly turned the water red. The water swirled around his head as the killer pushed down on the lever. He gave him an old fashioned swirlie.

Out of breath and exhausted, Kyle lifted his head out of the toilet—bloody water dripping from his sopping hair. He croaked and groaned, but he couldn't utter a word. It didn't matter anyway. His attacker wasn't planning on giving him a platform.

The masked man grabbed another fistful of his hair, then he thrust Kyle's head towards the rim of the toilet with all of his might. Kyle's nose was crushed upon impact. His face was slammed on the edge of the toilet again, causing the rim to crack. A gash formed on the bridge of his nose. Yet, the young man still clung to life.

So, the killer dunked Kyle's head into the water again. He disregarded his flailing limbs and the bubbling water. In fact, he pushed his head *deeper* into the bowl. He held his head under the water even after he stopped moving. He had to make sure he was dead. He counted the seconds and analyzed each involuntary twitch.

One, two, three... fifteen seconds—Kyle passed away. He was drowned in a toilet and his death was recorded on a cell phone.

The masked killer stopped the recording, then he shoved his phone into his coat pocket. He removed his gloves and mask, but he still hid his face under the hood of his raincoat. He casually exited the restroom, leaving Kyle in the toilet to be found by an unsuspecting classmate.

Chapter Seven

Evacuate

The students stared up at the ceiling as the fire alarm echoed through the school. Charlene glanced over at the neighboring group—Kyle had not yet returned. Michael stared back at Charlene and shrugged. The teacher approached the door and peeked into the hallway. Faculty members and students calmly exited their classrooms and followed the evacuation procedure.

The teacher returned to the classroom and said, "Okay. It looks like we'll be evacuating the campus. You know the drill. Stay calm, walk in a single-file line, and head to the field. Grab your stuff. Come on, let's go. I'll be right behind you."

As the students gathered their belongings and chattered, Charlene asked, "Is this a drill? Is it... Is it a *real* emergency?"

"I wasn't told about any drills before class, so treat it like the real deal. Go on, Charlene. I'm watching you."

Charlene grabbed her bag and followed her peers out of the classroom. She rushed to Michael's side, refusing to walk in a single-file line during the spontaneous evacuation. She watched as the students from the other classes filled the halls and marched to the emergency exits.

Charlene tugged on Michael's arm and asked, "What do you think happened?"

Michael pulled away from her grip and said, "It's probably nothing."

"You heard her back there. She said it wasn't a drill."

"If it's not a drill, then it's probably a kitchen fire. We wouldn't be *walking* out of here if it was a school shooter or a bomb threat. I think we'd be rushed out a lot faster than this if that was happening, right?"

Charlene stood on her tiptoes and examined the students ahead of her, then she glanced over her shoulder and did the same. The evacuation felt like a drill—there wasn't a sense of urgency or danger in the school. However, she was still suspicious of Kyle's absence.

Charlene said, "I don't know. It just doesn't feel right. Kyle leaves class for ten minutes, the alarm goes off, and now everyone's evacuating from the school... Something's wrong."

"You're over-thinking it, Charles. Something's always going to be wrong when you're never looking for what's right. Just move on."

Charlene was bothered by Michael's nonchalant attitude during the aftermath of seemingly endless tragedy. She tried her best to convince him of the dangers lurking in the city, but she needed irrefutable evidence to persuade him—*solid proof.*

And, they found that proof around the corner.

Charlene and Michael stopped at a fork in the road. The pair stared down the hallway to the left. To their utter surprise, the corridor was cordoned off by the police. Two cops stood at one end of the hall while two officers stood at the other end. The corridor appeared vacant. Students and faculty were not allowed to walk down that specific hallway.

While the other doors were closed, the boys' bathroom door remained opened. A police officer leaned on the doorway with his arms crossed. Booming voices could be heard from the bathroom, but the words were muffled.

Charlene asked, "Do you still think it's nothing?"

Michael responded, "No. I think it could be anything. An accident, a fight, a water leak... Come on, let's go."

He grabbed Charlene's wrist and pulled her away from the corridor. Charlene shambled forward, her eyes locked on the bathroom door. *Kyle went to the bathroom and now the bathroom is blocked,* she thought, *what other proof do you need?* She couldn't pull away from Michael's grip, though. The pair moved forward and followed the line.

The students found themselves outside. They formed several lines on the football field, each line representing a different classroom. Their teachers stood in front of the lines, counting heads and taking roll. A few police officers surrounded the field, too, trying to inconspicuously blend with the crowds. Of course, they stuck out like a billionaire reality star at a presidential debate.

As their teacher took roll, Charlene said, "Michael, I think it's serious. We wouldn't evacuate the school because of a fight or a flood in the bathroom."

"You're still over-thinking it," Michael responded.

"*I'm not.* I'm thinking logically. The police wouldn't be here if it wasn't something serious. Someone could have gotten seriously hurt and the killer might be on campus. Hell, the killer might be

Kyle and he–"

"*Stop it.* Just stop it, Charlene. I care about you, okay? I don't want you to worry about this because it's not that serious. This isn't a movie, alright? There isn't a big twist waiting around every corner. A killer isn't watching you from behind the hedges. Whatever happened... It didn't happen to us. That's all that matters. So, try to relax. *Please.*"

Charlene sighed in disappointment. She was stunned by Michael's selfish attitude, but she didn't attack him for it. Her relationship with Adam was already strained and she refused to burn another bridge. She stepped back and withdrew from the conversation. She glanced over to her right. Three classes down, she could see Britney in another line.

With half-a-smile, she stood on her tiptoes and waved at her close friend, trying her best to get her attention—and it worked. Her friend waved back at her. The pair were like twin sisters. They shared a very special connection. They could also read each other's lips and attitudes. They were both frustrated and hungry for information.

Charlene mouthed, "What happened?"

Britney shrugged and mouthed, "I don't know." She pointed at Charlene's teacher and mouthed, "Did she say anything?"

Charlene frowned and shook her head—*nope.* She glanced over at her teacher. She already finished taking roll, so she was talking with the other faculty members—presumably about the incident. She couldn't read their lips. She slinked away from her class and approached Britney.

She asked, "You haven't heard anything?"

Britney shook her head and said, "No. Why? Did you hear something?"

"No. I... I saw something, though."

"What?"

"It's probably nothing, but... I saw Kyle leave our class. He went to the bathroom."

"*So?*" Britney responded, confused.

Charlene explained, "Well, he went to the bathroom, but he didn't come back. When we were evacuating from the school, I noticed one of the bathrooms in a hallway was blocked by the police. There were more of them inside the bathroom, too. I know it."

Britney furrowed her brow and nodded as she lowered her head and stared at the grass. She quickly connected the pieces.

She asked, "You think something happened to Kyle? Or... Or do you think Kyle did something?"

Charlene didn't have an answer for Britney. There were dozens of possible conclusions to the scenario. She didn't believe Kyle killed Tiffany since it was physically impossible according to the rumors she heard, but she believed he was hiding something. She needed information from a trusted source in order to formulate a plausible theory.

Fortunately, Wilson walked across the field with a clipboard in his hands. He finished his roll-call, so he was going to mingle with the other teachers.

Charlene said, "Come on. Let's ask Wilson." The pair hurriedly walked between the students and approached the front of the line. Charlene shouted, "Mr. Wilson!"

Wilson stopped and glanced back at the girls. He appeared distraught, hollow-eyed and pale-faced as if he had just seen a ghost. He glanced back at the other teachers. For a moment, he thought about ignoring his students. He couldn't muster the courage to walk away from them, though. He respected them and they respected him.

Wilson asked, "How can I help you, ladies?"

Charlene asked, "What are we doing out here? Huh? What the hell happened in *there?* Is someone hurt?"

"I don't know all of the details. I–"

"What do you know?" Charlene interrupted.

Wilson stared at Charlene with a set of worried eyes, trying to dissuade her from pursuing the subject. To his dismay, the student was persistent. He stared down at the grass and rubbed the nape of his neck as he contemplated his response.

He said, "I... I can't tell you anything, Charlene. I know you're curious and scared, but I *can't* run my mouth about this. You're just going to have to wait out here until your parents pick you up."

Britney asked, "Does that mean school is over? I mean, do we have practice today for cheerleading, baseball, football... *anything?*"

"School is over... for now," Wilson responded, disappointed. As he walked away, he said, "Go back to your lines and wait for your parents. Everything's going to be okay."

Charlene and Britney glanced over at each other, baffled and terrified. A significant reason would be required to close the school—and it could be anything. Without any other useful options, they returned to their lines and waited for their guardians.

Chapter Eight

Home Sweet Home

Charlene lay on her bed, sunset sunshine pouring through the neighboring window. She vacantly stared at the dusty ceiling as she thought about the incident at school. *Kyle was attacked by the killer,* she thought, *or Kyle killed someone in the bathroom.* She created several scenarios in her mind, but she couldn't find a reasonable conclusion without all of the pieces to the puzzle.

She coughed and turned on her bed, kicking and squirming like a child throwing a temper tantrum at the mall. She stared at her dresser across the room. Photos of her friends clung to the mirror on the dresser. The images—from school events, local fairs, and group trips—brought a tear to her eye. She felt as if they were all in danger and she couldn't do anything to stop it. Helplessness was the most debilitating sensation.

A buzzing sound emerged in the room.

Charlene glanced at the nightstand next to her bed. Under the lamp, her cell phone moved an inch with each vibration. The caller ID read: *Anonymous.* She sat up in bed and answered the phone, hesitant.

She said, "Hello. *Hello?*" There was no response. She asked, "Adam, did you get a new number? Are you messing with me? Michael? Stephen?"

Yet again, no one answered.

Charlene glanced over her shoulder. She leaned

back on her bed and stared out her window. She could see the neighboring house and the street. A few kids wandered the street, oblivious of the murderer lurking in the city. She didn't see a masked killer in a raincoat watching her from afar, though.

Charlene said, "I'm going to call the police. Anonymous calling doesn't mean shit. They'll track it and–"

She paused upon hearing hoarse breathing on the line. The croaky breathing continued for twenty seconds, as if the caller were having trouble breathing.

In a deep synthesized voice, the caller said, "You didn't help him... No, you didn't hurt him, but you didn't *help* him. It's the same thing, isn't it? It's the same damn thing."

"What are you–"

"*Shut up!* Shut your slutty little mouth!" the caller barked. He cackled deliriously, causing his voice synthesizer to malfunction. As he recomposed himself, the caller said, "I... *I* know about the pain. A child shouldn't have to feel that pain. You kids... You fucking kids... It seems harmless on the surface, just games and words, but it burns and it burns until there's nothing left to burn. Oh, God, if you only knew that pain..."

Charlene furrowed her brow as the caller whimpered. His shifts in mood were eerie. Yet, she allowed the call to continue.

The caller said, "Well, I'm going to show the world what the world showed him."

Charlene asked, "What are you talking about?"

The caller remained silent. Only his raspy

breathing emerged on the phone. A *crackling* sound accompanied the breathing.

Before Charlene could say another word, a group of overlapping synthesized voices shouted: *Loser! Loner! Punk! Snitch! Bitch! Asshole! Freak! Cocksucker! Faggot! Kill yourself!*

Charlene pulled the phone away from her ear, shocked. She stared at the screen as the overlapping voices continued to play through the speakers. The raspy, crackling voices sounded as if they were in pain, like animals in a slaughterhouse. She recognized the harsh words, though. The call disconnected before she could respond.

She lowered the phone and stared at her lap, awed. The creepy phone call sent her into a tailspin of doubt. She thought: *it was just a prank, right?* She grimaced in disgust and her stomach turned as she thought about it. The message was ominous, the words were hurtful. The insults didn't appear to be targeting her, but it still made her feel uncomfortable.

She sent a text message to Britney. The message read: *I just got the WEIRDEST call, Brit. I'm scared.*

Britney quickly responded: *Call the cops!!* Before Charlene could type a response, Britney sent another message that read: *Or maybe it was just a prank? Did you ask the boys?*

Charlene responded: *I can't ask Adam. He doesn't have service. I don't know if it was the others. What should I do?*

The young woman sighed, then she pouted as she waited for her friend's response. She didn't expect Britney to respond immediately anyway. She presented her best friend with a complicated problem, so she didn't expect her to form a thorough solution within seconds. Her phone buzzed as she received another message.

Britney responded: *Tell your parents?*

Charlene sighed as she composed her response. The message read: *Mom is at the school meeting. Dad is sleeping. I don't wanna wake him before his night shift.*

Britney responded: *Shit. I don't know what to tell you.* (Her text message was followed by a sad emoji.)

Charlene responded: *Don't worry about it. I'll tell them later. I guess I'm just really nervous.*

She lowered her cell phone and stared at the doorway. She could see the hallway from her bed. The home was quiet—a creaky floorboard here, a groaning pipe there. She could hear her father's snoring down the hall. The man was knocked out, but she still felt safe around him. His presence was reassuring.

As she thought about the call, Charlene whispered, "Adam, Michael, Stephen... *Kyle.* It could be any one of them. Shit, it could even be a girl." She stared at her phone and said, "You didn't hurt him, but you didn't help him... What does it mean?"

She gasped and hopped as a *clacking* sound emerged from over her shoulder. She quickly staggered off of her bed and glanced back at the window. She sighed in relief upon spotting Adam standing on her father's ladder outside of her bedroom.

Adam smiled and said, "Open the window. Come on, I don't want to fall out here."

As she opened the window, Charlene said, "I should push you off for acting like such an asshole."

Adam climbed through the window and crawled across her bed, then he sat at the edge of the mattress—nonchalant, as if he weren't breaking the house rules.

Charlene asked, "What are you doing here? You scared me."

"Scared you? I always come through your window. What's the big deal?"

Charlene crossed her arms and stared down at the floorboards, visibly anxious. She wanted to tell him about the call, but she didn't know if she could trust him. She only allowed him into her home because of her father's presence. Otherwise, she probably would have pushed him off of the ladder and let him spend a night at the hospital.

She said, "My dad's been working the night shift recently. I don't want you to wake him up. I want him to rest and you know he doesn't like it when you're here without his permission."

Adam chuckled, then he responded, "So, your dad is knocked out right now? Shit, I could have just walked through the front door." He beckoned to his girlfriend and said, "Come on, sit down with me. Don't worry, I'll be very, *very* quiet."

Charlene stared at Adam with a deadpan expression, then she burst into a gentle giggle. She held her hands over her cheeks and blushed. She couldn't resist her boyfriend's charm. Despite their arguments—a rocky year riddled with fights—she still loved him.

The couple sat next to each other on the bed.

They shared a long, passionate kiss. Adam rubbed the nape of Charlene's neck while Charlene caressed Adam's clean-shaved jaw. One thing led to another and Adam's hand ended up on Charlene's chest. He gently squeezed her breast and leaned forward, trying to push her down to the mattress.

Charlene pulled away from Adam's lips, then she stood from the bed. She shimmied as she organized her clothing. She thought about having sex with Adam to relieve her stress, but she couldn't go through with it. Death and dick didn't blend well in her mind.

Adam asked, "What's wrong? You said your dad was sleeping, right? The man sleeps like a fucking bear. We could fuck on top of his body and he wouldn't notice. Come on, let's have some fun. It's been a while, you know..."

Stony-faced, Charlene shook her head and said, "No. No, I can't. I can't just have sex with you with... with *everything* that's been happening. People are dying, Adam, and it just doesn't feel right." She rubbed her eyes and swiped at her nose as she sniffled. She paced back-and-forth and said, "I think it's Kyle. I got a phone call earlier from some creep. I don't know what he was talking about, but everything else leads to Kyle. Even if he didn't kill Tiffany, he could have killed Anna. He's hiding something and he could be coming after us. I just know it."

"Charlene, it wasn't Kyle," Adam said. Charlene stopped pacing and stared at her boyfriend, baffled. Adam explained, "I heard a rumor when we were evacuating from the school. Some guys were talking about some other freshman that went into a bathroom near the English classes. They said that kid saw Kyle in there."

"S–So?"

"He was dead. I don't know how he died, but, if that rumor is true, then *he's dead.* There's nothing to worry about. So, we can, you know, mess around a little."

As Adam grabbed her wrist, Charlene shook her head and said, "No. Just... Just stop it. I'm not doing this right now, Adam." She pulled away from his grip and stepped in reverse until she reached her dresser. She said, "If Kyle is dead, that means there really is a serial killer out there. The killer is clearly targeting students, too—students like us. We're not safe. He could be anyone. I mean, he... he could even be you."

"*Me?*" Adam repeated in disbelief. He nervously chuckled, then he asked, "Why would you think I'm the killer?"

"I don't know. Your phone is 'conveniently' out of service, you showed up late to school today, you showed up here right after I got that call, and... and you've just been so distant recently. I don't Think I even know who you are anymore."

Adam watched as his girlfriend sniveled, disheartened. Like Charlene, he still loved her despite their fighting. He cared about her well-being. His sexual urges often controlled him, but he wouldn't allow sex to destroy his relationship.

Adam said, "Don't talk like that, Charles. I'm sorry. I'm... I'm sorry for everything. It's been a rough year, I know. We can make it better, though. Sit down. Let's talk about this."

Charlene stared at Adam with a raised brow, caught off guard by his understanding attitude. She sat down beside him, then she leaned on his shoulder. Adam pushed her hair away from her face, then he wrapped his arm around her body. His macho personality wouldn't allow him to admit it, but he felt comfortable around her—like a newborn baby with his mother.

Adam asked, "So, who do you think did it?"

Charlene stared up at Adam and said, "I don't know. I just don't know. I really thought it was Kyle. It could be anyone. A student, a parent, a teacher, a cop..."

"We need a lead. If we want to find out who's killing everyone, we need to get away from this dead end."

"Where can we find another 'lead?' We're not cops, Adam."

"Yeah, but we can ask the only person who actually spoke to the cops—*Melanie.* She has to know something, right?"

Charlene leaned away from her boyfriend. She gazed into Adam's eyes, analyzing the sincerity behind his words. *Does he know something I don't?*– she thought.

Charlene asked, "Are you saying you want to go talk to Melanie? *Right now?*"

"Yeah. If this is really bothering you, then we have to get to the bottom of it. Let's sneak into Melanie's house and talk to her. She lives like three, maybe four blocks away. Let's go."

Charlene clenched her jaw and glanced around the room as she seriously considered the suggestion.

Her eyes stopped at the doorway. She could still hear her father's snoring. The thought of betraying her parents' trust killed her. However, the thought of actually dying at the hands of a serial killer was much more worrisome.

Charlene said, "Okay, I'll go. Let me just grab my jacket."

Chapter Nine

Like House Arrest

"Come on, just jump," Adam hissed.

Charlene sat atop the brick wall in the backyard, the sun setting behind her. She glanced back at the alleyway behind her—there was no turning back. She took a deep breath, then she leaped off of the wall. The young woman grunted as she landed on the grass beside Adam, teetering as she struggled to keep her footing.

Adam grabbed her arm and said, "I told you it wouldn't hurt."

"Yeah, yeah," Charlene muttered.

She swiped at the dirt on her skirt and stared at the one-story house directly ahead. The little red house belonged to Melanie and her family. A police cruiser with one police officer was parked in front of the house, so the teenagers decided to enter the home through the back.

Adam approached the back door. He peeked into the house through the glass panes on the door. He found himself staring into a hallway. A few of the rooms appeared to be illuminated, but no one was walking through the home.

Charlene asked, "How do we get inside?"

Disregarding the question, Adam slowly turned the door knob. To his utter surprise, the door was unlocked. He pushed the door open and stood in the doorway. He could hear the local news from a television in the living room down the hall.

With a devious smirk on his face, Adam joked, "She thinks she's about to be killed, so she leaves her back door open... Real bright, Melanie." He glanced over at Charlene and whispered, "Have you been here before?"

Charlene nodded and whispered, "Yeah, once or twice."

"Which one is her room?"

Charlene peeked into the hall. She whispered, "It was, um... the second door to the right."

"Good. Let's move in real fast. As soon as we're in there, I'm going to cover her mouth so she doesn't scream. You explain everything to her. We don't want to get caught here."

Charlene nodded in agreement. The couple crept into the small home, walking with their heels and shoulders raised. They peeked through an archway to the left—the kitchen was dark and it looked like it was empty. Shadows swallowed the other end of the room. They ignored the first door on the right. From the second door to the right, they could see the living room to the left.

Melanie's mother, a frail brunette woman, sat on a sofa in the living room, a blue robe draped over her body. A stack of envelopes sat on the glass coffee table in front of her; a cup of wine sat beside the stack. The woman appeared stressed, focused on her bills. The sensationalized news—which always focused on the worst of humanity—was loud enough to mask all of the noise in the house.

Adam leaned closer to Charlene's ear and whispered, "Remember: *move fast.*"

Charlene nodded, determined. Adam tightly gripped the door knob. He stared at Charlene and nodded three times—one, two, three, *go!* The door swung open.

Eyes full of fear, Melanie quickly turned on her bed and stared at the door. She gasped and opened her mouth to shriek. Adam swiftly lunged towards Melanie's bed—three wide strides. He covered her mouth and wrapped his other arm around her body, then he rolled onto the bed. He physically stopped her from screaming, but he still shushed her.

During the struggle, Charlene slipped into the room and quietly closed the door behind her. She approached the wrestling pair with her index finger over her lips—*please, be quiet.*

She whispered, "Melanie, it's Charlene and Adam. We're not here to hurt you. Please, keep it down. *Please.*" She gently caressed Melanie's face, wiping the tears from her rosy cheeks. She whispered, "We're not going to hurt you. We just need your help."

As if she were calmed by her gentle touch, Melanie loosened up. She stopped resisting Adam's grip and she stopped whimpering. She nodded at Charlene, communicating without uttering a word— *I understand.*

Adam removed his hand from Melanie's mouth, then he slid out from under her body. He whispered, "I'm sorry. We knew you'd scream and we didn't want to cause a scene."

As Adam stood from the bed, Melanie crawled across her mattress until her back hit the wall. She stared at the intruding couple, baffled by their presence in her home. Although she only saw one murderer in the video chat, she didn't trust either one of them.

Melanie asked, "What are you doing here?"

Charlene responded, "I... I don't know how to explain this. It kind of seems... I don't know, it seems really stupid now that we're here."

"We want to know about Tiffany's murder," Adam said. "I'm really not interested in it, I don't think it's any of our business, but Charlene is worried and I don't like that. So, we came here to ask you about it since you 'supposedly' saw it. What do you know, Melanie?"

Melanie stared at Adam, then she glanced at Charlene. She gazed into Charlene's lustrous eyes, hypnotized by the fear tormenting her benevolent soul. The pair were acquaintances at school, sharing a chat here and there. They weren't deeply connected, so she wondered why Charlene would be worried about the killer.

Melanie nodded and said, "You should be worried about him. You don't want to end up like Tiffany."

Charlene asked, "What really happened to her?"

"She was... She was killed. I guess you know that already, but, I mean... she was *slaughtered.* God, I still can't believe it."

Melanie held her trembling hands over her face as she whimpered. Tears streamed across her cheeks and mucus filled her nostrils. The terrifying memories broke her heart.

Her voice cracking, she said, "A person hid in her closet while she was looking for something. When she came back, the... the person came out of her closet and killed her. He... He... He *ripped* her jaw off. He really did. He–He almost cut her tongue off, too. He did it all with a knife. Only a knife... It was just like the rumors of Anna's death, except... I actually saw it."

Charlene held her hand over her gaping mouth while Adam furrowed his brow and took a step in reverse. The couple were disgusted by the gruesome details.

Eyes welling over with tears, Charlene stuttered, "Wha–What did he look like? The killer... What did he look like? Kyle told me he was wearing a coat and a mask. Do you remember that?"

Melanie responded, "Well, Kyle wasn't lying. I remember everything. He wore a black raincoat and his hood covered his hair. He wore a mask, too. It was like a... a normal paper-mâché mask, but it was painted. Lipstick on the lips, eye-shadow around the eyes, and... and blood on his cheeks. Maybe it was red paint, but I'm sure it was supposed to be blood. It looked like some kid painted it. It was so creepy..."

Charlene bit her bottom lip as she thought about the description. The raincoat reminded her of the person she saw before school. The mask sounded familiar, too. *Like a child painted it,* she thought, *didn't someone paint masks at school?* She couldn't put her finger on a specific face, though.

Disrupting Charlene's contemplation, Melanie said, "I don't trust anyone... not even myself. Since last night, since Tiffany's murder, I've been afraid of everything and everyone. I can't stand being alone, but I can't stand being with anyone else, either. Any noise I hear, every shadow I see... I think it could be him. Whoever 'he' is..." She glanced over at Adam and said, "It could even be you."

Adam cocked his head back, astonished by the allegation. He asked, "What? Why me? Why not Charlene?"

"Charlene and Tiffany are... *were* the same size. The person who killed Tiffany was bigger and stronger than her. He was a man. I know that for sure... I don't know who it could be, though. He could be some random psycho. He could be a parent, a cop, a teacher. I don't know."

A teacher—the idea echoed through Charlene's mind, clouding her skull and flooding the crevices of her brain. She quickly sorted through her past teachers while considering each piece of evidence in the murders. She eliminated the female teachers and focused on the mask. Her eyes widened as the thought dawned onto her.

Charlene said, "I don't think I ever saw a mask like that, but I remember seeing weird drawings on a piece of paper on Wilson's desk. I saw them there a few times in our sophomore and junior years. Kind of like... like bloody, *warped* smiley faces."

Melanie nodded and said, "It could be him. He's big, he's strong, and he knows us... He could be killing his students for some sick, demented reason. You know, I heard he likes young girls, so, *who knows...* I'd stay away from him if I were you."

"No, we should get closer to him," Adam said. Charlene stared at her boyfriend with a set of wide, protuberant eyes that said: *really?* Adam continued, "Yeah. We've already gone this far. I know where Wilson lives, too. I can call Michael and tell him to pick us up, then we'll stake out Wilson's house. We can get to the bottom of this."

Charlene puckered her lips as she considered the suggestion. She glanced over at Melanie and frowned. Melanie's sorrowful eyes spoke volumes about her opinion on the matter. If Wilson was the killer, they would be walking right into his clutches.

Charlene said, "We'll watch his house for an hour or two. If we see anything suspicious, we call the police. Okay?"

Adam said, "Deal. Can I use your phone to call Michael?" As Charlene handed her phone to him, Adam said, "One last thing: if it's not Wilson, I think it would be smart if we dropped this. Okay? Catching our *possibly* crazy teacher is one thing, catching a *real* serial killer is a whole different monster... I'll meet you outside."

Charlene watched as Adam quietly crept out of the room. She turned her attention to her traumatized classmate. Melanie glanced every which way as she listened to every creak in the house and each whoosh outside. She couldn't control her anxiety, she couldn't trump her fears.

Charlene said, "We'll leave now, Melanie. Well, unless you want me to stay and–"

"Just go," Melanie interrupted. "I don't want anything to do with you, with Adam, or with that psycho out there. Just go. Leave me alone."

"Okay, okay. I'm sorry for... for everything."

Charlene cracked a nervous smile and waved at Melanie. Her classmate didn't acknowledge her, so she reluctantly crept out of the room. She ignored the living room, completely avoiding Melanie's mother, then she escaped through the back door. She met with Adam in the backyard, then the couple hopped over the brick wall. They jogged back to the street, eager to meet Michael and continue their investigation.

Chapter Ten

Revelations

The buzzing lamp posts, the full moon, and the glittering stars illuminated the cold streets—the sun had already fallen. A few people wandered the suburban streets after dark, casually strolling down the tree-lined sidewalks. A black sedan sat at the corner of an intersection. The vehicle offered the perfect view of a beige two-story house near the corner.

In the car, Michael sat in the driver's seat, Adam sat in the passenger's seat, and Charlene sat in the back. The friends kept their eyes locked on the beige house.

Michael yawned, then he asked, "What are we doing here again?"

Adam said, "I told you already: we just want to watch Wilson for a few hours."

"Why?"

Charlene explained, "It's a long story, but we think Wilson might have something to do with all of the murders recently."

Michael stared at Charlene through the rear-view mirror, watching her with a deadpan expression. He huffed and shook his head, simultaneously amused and bothered by the explanation.

He said, "I told you: if you keep digging, you might get buried. What makes you think Wilson, our math teacher, is a killer? Huh? He's a fucking math nerd,

Charles! He doesn't have what it takes to kill someone, especially one of his own students. You've seen how he looks at every girl in his class, man. He couldn't kill 'em..."

Charlene responded, "Like I said, it's a long story. I've been through this with Adam and we both agree: he *could* be the killer. If not, he might lead us to him."

"Why do you want to find the killer so badly? I mean, do you really think he'd go after you?"

"I don't know. All I know is: he's killed three students and he's not showing any signs of stopping. I'm scared and I need to know what I'm scared of. Okay?"

Michael dug his fingers into his hair, frustrated. He couldn't help but chuckle as he thought about the situation. *Staking out a house like a bunch of amateur detectives,* he thought, *it's like we're kids all over again.*

He asked, "Well, what makes you think it was Wilson? Tell me the long story."

"Melanie said the killer was a big man, *like Wilson.* And, she told us about the killer's mask."

"What about it?"

"It had a very specific design. It had all this messed up make-up on it. It looked like it had blood on its cheeks, like if it was... *crying* blood. She said it looked like a child painted it. I remember seeing a drawing like that on Wilson's desk. It was a weird design. I don't remember who drew it, though."

"Like a child painted it," Michael repeated, curious. "I think I remember seeing something like that, too. Wasn't it–"

"Get down, here he comes," Adam interrupted.

The friends sank into their seats as a black sedan rolled past them. The car pulled into the driveway of the beige house. The driver wasn't alone, though. Another person sat in the passenger seat—and the pair appeared to be flirting.

Adam asked, "Wilson isn't married, is he?"

Without taking her eyes off of the car, Charlene responded, "No, he's not."

Wide-eyed, Michael leaned forward and stared at the car. As expected, Wilson climbed out of the driver's seat. To his utter surprise, Dominique hopped out of the passenger seat. He watched as his girlfriend embraced the teacher.

In the driveway, barely hidden by the shadows, Wilson and Dominique shared a kiss—a quick peck on the lips. Wilson chuckled as Dominique blushed. The pair acted like a normal high school couple.

Wilson could be heard saying, "Not here, not here."

Awed, Michael said, "She was supposed to be home. She–She said her parents weren't letting her go out tonight. She... She said she wasn't going out!"

Charlene said, "Michael, calm down. Please, don't–"

Disregarding his friend's pleas, Michael pushed his door open and hopped out of his car. Caught in his emotions, he didn't care if he caused a scene in the tranquil neighborhood. He ran across the street, then he effortlessly vaulted over Wilson's fence.

Dominique gasped upon spotting her furious boyfriend. She slinked behind Wilson, hiding behind his shoulder. Rosy-cheeked, Wilson lifted his hands over his head as if he were just caught by the police. His worst nightmare came true—he was caught in a relationship with his student.

Michael stopped in front of the disloyal couple. The young man was rendered speechless due to his anger. He wanted to take a swing at his teacher, but he stopped himself. Adam and Charlene pushed the gate open and ran onto Wilson's front lawn.

Wilson stuttered, "We–We... We weren't doing anything. Oh, shit... Wha–What are you doing here?"

Michael jabbed his index finger at Wilson and asked, "What are *you* doing with my girlfriend? Huh?" He leaned to his right and glared at Dominique. He barked, "What are you doing with him?! Huh? What the hell are you doing here, Dom?"

Wilson waved and said, "Please, keep it down, Michael. It's... It's not what it looks like. Please, let's just... let's just talk about this inside."

"Inside? *Inside?* What? Are you too embarrassed to talk about this out here? Is that it? You don't want your neighbors to hear about your relationship with a high school kid?! Is that it?!"

The neighbors' porch lights turned on. The nosy neighbors were drawn to the drama, watching from their windows and peepholes.

Wilson held his hand over his face, ashamed. Teary-eyed, Dominique buried her face in Wilson's back and sobbed.

Michael extended his arms away from his body and shouted, "Look! My teacher is fucking my girlfriend! My *seventeen*-year-old girlfriend! This fucking pervert is... is..." He sighed and shook his head, unable to continue his rant. He whispered,

"He's really fucking my girlfriend."

As she grabbed his wrist, Charlene said, "I'm sorry, Michael. We shouldn't have–"

"*Stop.* Just stop it," Michael interrupted. He pulled away from Charlene's grip and walked past the gate. Without looking back, he shouted, "Don't call me, Dominique!"

Adam leaned on the fence and said, "Michael, don't go. Come on, man. Where are you going?"

"I'm going to blow off some steam! Take a bus home or something! Don't call me, either!"

The group watched as Michael hopped into his car. His wheels howled as he peeled out and zoomed away.

Adam glanced back at the group and said, "He's probably going to the baseball field to cool off. Don't worry, he's going to be alright. He'll bounce back."

Wilson loudly swallowed the lump in his throat, then he said, "I shouldn't be doing this, but... you can come in if you want. I'll explain everything... although it may not be necessary. Come on."

Wilson nodded at the couple, then he strolled up the walkway. Dominique stared at Adam and Charlene—shame sitting on one shoulder, guilt sitting on the other. She nodded at her friends, then she followed the teacher.

Charlene and Adam glanced at each other. They didn't have any other options, so they followed Wilson into his home.

***

The group gathered in the living room of Wilson's house. Adam, Charlene, and Dominique awkwardly sat on a three-seat sofa while Wilson sat on a recliner. The sofa and the recliner were separated by a coffee table. Three mugs filled with coffee sat on the table—one for each student. The teenagers weren't eager to drink his coffee, though.

Her hands under her thighs, Charlene glanced around the living room. There were a few framed family pictures on the walls above the console tables and desks. None of the images were recent, though. The living room was *very* clean and organized, too. She assumed Wilson had some sort of obsessive-compulsive disorder. The home had an eerie aura to it—something was afoot.

Breaking the silence, Wilson said, "So, I guess it's obvious: Dominique and I are in a... a relationship. It's... It's not a *sexual* relationship. I mean, we've had sex, but that's not what it's about. I'm not taking advantage of her and she's not taking advantage of me. It's about love. Okay? It's about *forbidden* love. And, since it's forbidden, I hope we can keep this a secret between us. Please."

Charlene and Adam glanced at each other, anxious. The couple sought answers to a murder mystery, they weren't interested in an immoral love triangle.

Twiddling her thumbs, Dominique said, "He's right. I've heard the rumors in school. 'Some cheerleader is dating Wilson so she can get better grades.' That's not true. I'm doing fine in school already. It's real love. I didn't want you guys to find out this way. I was going to wait until after we all graduated. I would have turned eighteen right after and everything would have been... *kinda* normal."

Charlene sighed, then she said, "Listen, this is

serious, but there are more important issues going on right now. Okay? We didn't come here to catch you cheating. We didn't even know you were going to be here, Dom. We came here to ask questions."

"About what?" Wilson asked.

"About the murders. I remember seeing drawings on your desk during my sophomore year. I think I even saw them last year. They were drawn on worksheets. They were kinda childish and kinda creepy. Do you remember them? Hmm? Who drew them? Why did you have them?"

"Drawings? I'm... I'm not exactly sure what you're talking about, Charlene. Students doodle on their worksheets all the time. What does that have to do with the murders?"

Adam explained, "Melanie described the killer's mask to us. It was a creepy mask with a lot of make-up and bloody tears."

Wilson puckered his lips and glanced up at the ceiling as he thought about the description. He sighed and shook his head as the thought dawned onto him—it wasn't pretty.

He said, "I think I know what you're talking about. First of all, they weren't just drawings on worksheets. They weren't doodles or anything like that. They *were* masks—masks made out of worksheets. I just unfolded some of them. That's probably what you saw. They were normal masks, mouth masks, and even, um... domino masks. Casey made them for me."

"Casey..." Dominique repeated, baffled.

"Yeah, *Casey Marshall.* You know, he... he made them before he took his own life last year."

The students glanced at each other upon hearing the name, awed by the revelation.

Casey Marshall was a student at their high school who committed suicide during the year prior. The frail teenager cut his wrists vertically, swallowed a bottle of sleeping pills, and hung himself in his closet. He did everything in his power to stop his family from reviving him. He wanted to permanently leave the cruel world.

Wilson continued, "I don't know if you knew him, but he was sort of the artistic-type. He sat at the back of class and kept to himself. He was... *enigmatic.* He gave me those masks when we spoke about the bullying he was going through. I guess they were supposed to be some sort of gift."

With a set of sharp, furious eyes, Dominique asked, "What did he say to you, Wilson?"

"Wha–What do you mean?"

"When he talked about the 'bullying' or whatever, what did he say? Did he say any names? Hmm? Why was he talking to *you?*"

Wilson raised his brow and scratched his hair, baffled by the defensive questioning. He glanced over at the other students—Charlene and Adam wanted answers, too.

Wilson said, "No... No, he didn't say any names. Casey just told me about the bullying. He told me about the name-calling, the fights, and the... the *molestation*—for lack of a better word. He told me how a few students disrobed him and recorded him. It was shocking stuff. He never said any names, though. He was afraid of retaliation, I suppose."

He sighed as he looked back on his relationship

with Casey. *Failure, disappointment*—the feelings made him sniffle. Casey went to him for help, but he wasn't able to save him. He didn't participate in the abuse, but he still felt guilty.

Noticing the students' silence, Wilson asked, "Did... Did any of you bully him?"

Wide-eyed, the students glanced at each other. Adam appeared to be surprised. Charlene looked sad and remorseful—a set of glum eyes and a frown on her face. Lost in a tailspin of emotions, Dominique appeared angry, sad, and confused.

Adam said, "I didn't know Casey, Wilson. I knew about him getting bullied, I left a few comments on some Facebook posts, but I didn't really do anything to hurt him. I definitely wasn't trying to get the kid to kill himself."

"I knew about the bullying, too," Charlene confessed. "I didn't do anything to him, though. I mean, I didn't even know it was that serious. I would have tried to do something if I knew."

Wilson, Adam, and Charlene turned their attention to Dominique. Dominique squirmed to the edge of the seat as she glanced at her friends.

The cheerleader stuttered, "It–It doesn't matter. *None* of this matters, okay? Melanie must have made a... a mistake. We're just assuming it was one of the masks Casey made. We–We're making something out of nothing. I mean, what are you thinking? A ghost is killing people? Huh? Casey's ghost is killing the people who bullied him? Is that it?"

Charlene responded, "It doesn't have to be something 'supernatural.' This isn't *Friday the 13th.* It could be one of Casey's friends or a family member, right?"

"*Wrong.* You're wrong, Charles. This is so fucking stupid!"

What's wrong with you? Did you–"

"Nothing's wrong with me, bitch! I'm just tired of talking about this! I'm sick and tired–"

"Alright, settle down," Wilson sternly said. The girls sank into their seats and retreated from the argument. Wilson said, "The cops are going to find this killer. It's *not* your job to investigate this. You don't know what type of trouble you can get yourself into by digging into the wrong places. So, here's what we'll do... I'll contact Sheriff Jackson and tell him about the masks. It's probably nothing, but I have to let him know. I'll tell him I got the information from an anonymous tip. I'll agree to keep quiet about all of your *possible* bullying and your snooping, too, if you agree to keep quiet about... about our little relationship. Do we have a deal? Adam? Charlene?"

Charlene and Adam glanced at each other, communicating with their eyes. Charlene's eyes said: *we have to keep digging.* Adam's eyes said: *this is our final stop, this is the end.*

Adam said, "We have a deal."

"Good. *Great.* I think you'll be able to convince Michael to keep this on the 'down-low.' At least, I hope so... Anyway, since he left in such a hurry, I'll give you guys a ride home. Let me get my keys."

Wilson nodded at the students, then he strolled into his kitchen. Dominique followed closely behind her lover, looking for a sense of reassurance.

Charlene grabbed Adam's arm and whispered, "I

don't think we should stop. We're still in danger and we can't trust anyone, remember?"

Adam responded, "We had an agreement. You promised we'd stop here, so we're stopping here."

"That's easy for you to say, Adam. You didn't get a call from the killer. And, that call matches with our theory. Someone might be trying to get vengeance—and he knows me. I could be next."

"Did he even say your name?"

Charlene asked, "What?"

Adam explained, "If he didn't say your name when you got the call, then he probably doesn't really know you. If it was the killer, he probably went through Tiffany's phone, copied all of the numbers, then randomly called everyone. There's nothing to worry about, okay? That person was just trying to scare you. He's trying to scare everyone. Just relax."

Charlene sighed in disappointment. She was disheartened by Adam's disregard for her safety. She found some comfort in his logical explanation, though. It made sense to her. She thought: *maybe he copied the numbers down and forgot to copy the names, maybe he doesn't actually know us.* She could only hope her boyfriend was correct.

The couple sat in silence, waiting for Wilson to drive them home.

Chapter Eleven

Baseball

Clang—the ringing metallic sound echoed through the quiet baseball field as Michael struck a ball with his aluminum bat. The ball flew over second base and soared into center field. No one was around to catch the ball at night, though. It landed on the grass, then it was pushed away by a gust of wind. The chilly breeze was welcomed during such a disappointing night.

As he grabbed another ball from the ground beside home plate, Michael muttered, "Dominique, you fucking whore... What were you thinking? Why would you fuck him? Why would you do this to me?" He wiped the tears from his eyes with the back of his hand. He stared at the twinkling stars above and said, "I'm going to get you back for this. I'm going to tell everyone about both of you, then I'm going to fuck all of your friends. You stupid bitch..."

He tossed the ball into the air, then he swung— *whoosh.* He missed by an inch. He watched as the ball bounced on the ground beneath him, irked. He rarely missed the ball, especially when he was practicing by himself, but there was too much on his mind. He couldn't concentrate.

He lifted the bat over his head, then he swung down at the ground. He felt the vibration in his arms as the bat collided with the floor. He hit the floor again and again—*and again.* It was a tried-and-tested exercise for relieving stress.

As the bat *clanged* with each strike, Michael shouted, "Damn it! Why would you do this to me?! You damn slu–"

He stopped, the tip of the bat hovering a foot over the ground. Over his frantic pummeling and screaming, he heard a person snickering—a soft, devious laughter. At that moment, it became clear to him: *he wasn't alone.*

Michael glanced over at the dugout and asked, "Who's there?"

No one answered.

He stood on his tiptoes and stared at the dugout, curious. Despite the darkness, he could see a silhouette in the shadowy corner of the dugout. Although nothing was certain—it could have been a forgotten uniform—he swore he saw the bottom of a person's raincoat and a pair of legs.

Michael cocked the bat over his shoulder and slowly approached the dugout. Anger flowing through his veins due to Dominique's cheating, the young man—a baseball player with a promising future—was ready to kill anyone in his path. He wouldn't bat an eye if he killed a homeless man as long as he released the rage in his system.

He stopped and said, "I'm having a bad day, man. If you want to do something, *do it.* I dare you, pussy." There was no response. Anxious, he took one step in reverse and said, "I'm batting .360, man. I'll knock your head off. You hear me? I'm... I don't really feel like spending a night in jail, though, so... just stay down. Don't test me."

Again, the snickering emerged from the dugout.

Before Michael could say another word, the figure stepped forward and hurled a ball at the baseball player. The baseball hit the tip of his nose—a direct hit. The ball broke Michael's nose, causing blood to spew from his nostrils. He staggered every which way, dazed by the unexpected hit.

As Michael teetered left-and-right, a person emerged from the shadows in the dugout. The person wore steel-toe boots, black jeans, and a matching raincoat. His face was veiled by a paper-mâché Bauta mask—a mask without a mouth hole. The mask had an angry expression, too. Just like the other masks, the mask was decorated with smeared lipstick and bloody tears.

Michael blinked erratically as he tried to focus his blurred vision. He saw triple, then double. He stared at his attacker, shocked. He noticed the camera strapped to his forehead—he was being recorded. He was more concerned with the masked person's weapon, though. The killer held a spiked baseball bat in his right hand. Dozens of rusty nails protruded from the wooden bat.

Michael stuttered, "S–Shit. Pl–Please, don't... don't hurt me."

Disregarding the pleas, the masked person struck Michael's right knee with all of his might. The nails penetrated his jeans and skin. The nails even scraped his bone. Michael howled as the insufferable pain surged through his body. He whimpered as he stared down at his blood-soaked jeans—the rusty nails were jammed in his leg.

Michael staggered down to his one good knee, crippled by the blow. The masked killer placed his boot on Michael's left ankle, then he tugged on the bat. He ignored his victim's bloodcurdling screams and indecipherable stammering. He was only concerned with retrieving his baseball bat.

He tightly gripped the handle, then he pulled back on the bat with all of his weight and force. *Squelching* and *shredding* sounds emerged over the crying as the nails ripped through his kneecap. The killer swung the bat down away from Michael, causing blood to splatter on the chalk line.

As he crawled away, eyes full of tears and mouth overflowing with saliva, Michael pleaded, "Don't do this! Please, don't hurt me! I'm sorry! I'll leave! Please, *I'll leave!*" His eyes widened as the killer approached him. As he stood on one foot and hopped away, Michael cried, "No, no, no! Please!"

Michael yelped as the killer struck his other leg with the bat. He missed his knee, though. Instead, he struck his shin. The nails still penetrated his pants and skin, though. The sheer force caused his entire leg to wobble, too. His tibia cracked with the pressure. The baseball player collapsed, landing face-first on home plate. With both of his legs mangled, he was effectively paralyzed by the attacker.

Michael rolled onto his back and held his arm up, as if he were blocking the light on a sunny day. He watched in fear as the killer towered over him. He couldn't see much due to his subtle clothing, but he could see his sharp, zany blue eyes. He saw sorrow, anger, and evil in his eyes—pure, *unadulterated* evil.

His voice cracking as if he were still going through puberty, Michael said, "Please, don't do this, man. I'm... I'm just a kid. I'm barely eighteen. I'll give you anything. You... You... You can take my car! Take it! I won't call the police, I won't tell anyone. Please, I'm begging you. I don't want to die. I don't–"

Mid-sentence, the masked person struck down at Michael's face with the spiked bat. Michael was silenced with the attack—*stunned.* A nail penetrated his left eye, which turned his eye red with blood. Tears of blood welled in his eyes, painting his eyelids red. Another nail penetrated his broken nose, piercing both of his nostrils and his nasal septum. Blood leaked from his nose and streamed down to his lips and chin. Three rusty nails were jammed into his cheek. The left side of his face was drenched in blood.

The killer placed his boot on Michael's chest, then he tugged on the bat. A *squishy* sound emerged as he shook the bat, trying to loosen it from the teenager's flesh. He rubbed his hands together, as if he were preparing to lift something heavy. He was playing with his victim—*teasing him.* He grabbed the bat with both hands, then, with one mighty yank, the killer pulled the bat and the nails out of his face.

He stared down at his victim's mutilated face as Michael twitched and squirmed. He was hurt, but he wasn't dead.

The masked killer held the bat over his head, then he swung down at Michael's face. He repeatedly hit the young man. Blood and bits of his flesh splattered on the field with each hit. One, two, three... *ten blows* —he stopped after the tenth strike, his heavy breaths escaping from under his mask. He leaned closer to his victim's mutilated face, recording every grisly detail.

Michael's head was caved in at the forehead. His cracked skull could be seen through the deep gashes left by the long, rusty nails—more holes than a block of Swiss cheese. His hair was soaked in blood. The rest of his face fared no better. Every inch of his face was covered in blood and riddled with lacerations. His right eye was closed while his other mutilated eyeball bulged *out* of his eye socket due to the sheer force of each hit. The eyeball dangled over his cheek.

The masked killer reached into Michael's pockets, searching for any valuables. He stole his cell phone and wallet. Satisfied with the murder, he stopped the recording and casually departed from the crime scene—leaving Michael's dead body on home plate.

Chapter Twelve

Live on Facebook

Charlene awoke to a jarring tune—an obnoxious, over-produced pop song disguised as a rap song. The song blared from her cell phone as the device vibrated across her nightstand. She grunted and whimpered, upset by the sudden awakening. The warm morning sunshine spilled into her room and caressed her body, but she didn't find any comfort in her home.

At heart, she despised the ringtone and the caller. She was plucked from a tender dream and dropped into a hellish nightmare.

As she sat up in bed, Charlene muttered, "Damn it. Who's calling at six in the morning?" She frowned as she stared at the name on her phone—*Britney.* Charlene answered, "Hey, Britney. What's going on?"

Britney asked, "Have you been on Facebook yet? Instagram? Twitter? *Anything?*"

"I just woke up. What is this about, Brit? You're scaring me..."

"Go to Facebook, Twitter... *anywhere,* and search: #ForCasey."

Charlene stuttered, "Ca–Casey...."

"C-a-s-e-y," Britney spelled the name. She said, "Search it. Someone live-streamed Melanie's murder and uploaded it online. It's going viral."

Charlene held her hand over her forehead, disoriented. She tightly closed her eyes and shook her head, struggling to keep her composure. The news struck her like a bus plowing over a stray animal. The name—*Casey*—stabbed at her brain.

She said, "Wait, wait, wait. Are you... Are you saying Melanie is dead? Melanie Myers?"

"Search it, Charlene. See for yourself."

"O–Okay... I'll call you back in a minute."

Charlene disconnected from the call. She grabbed her laptop from her nightstand and went to Facebook. She didn't have to search the term. Under the trending column, one of the trends read: *#ForCasey.* She took a deep breath, mentally preparing herself for the inevitable carnage, then she clicked on the trend.

From a quick glance, she could see the video was spreading like wildfire—social media users loved the macabre, although they would argue otherwise.

In each post, she could see Melanie on the thumbnail of the video players. A few users spoke cautiously about the video, warning others about the graphic content. Other users made crude comments about the video, claiming it was fake and joking about the content. A few paranoid users claimed the video was a 'distraction.'

Some small and fake news websites claimed it was a recording of a Facebook live-stream. The source didn't matter at the moment, though. The potential content bothered her the most.

Charlene pressed play on a video player and the video started.

The edited video depicted a person lurking outside of Melanie's home at night. The cameraman hid in the shadows next to the house, standing in plain sight. He even recorded the police cruiser parked in front of the house—the police failed to spot him. The cameraman turned his attention to Melanie, recording her through her bedroom window. His breathing could be heard over the blowing wind and rustling leaves. His husky breathing was eerie.

The video jump-cut to the cameraman using a lock-pick set to open the back door. He used both hands to use the pick and the rake, so Charlene assumed the camera was strapped onto his head. Upon unlocking the door, he quietly entered the home. He closed the door behind him, then he recorded the hallway. He peeked into the living room and found Melanie's mother still sitting on the sofa.

The video jump-cut again. The cameraman appeared to be standing still in the kitchen, hidden in the shadows. He had the perfect view of the living room through the archway to his left. He could see the hallway through the archway directly ahead, too. He moved his head to record the home, but he didn't move from his position.

As she watched the video, Charlene whispered, "What are you doing? What are you planning? Who–"

Her eyes widened with fear as she appeared in the footage. In the video, she followed Adam into the house. She saw herself glance into the kitchen, unaware of the other intruder's presence. Their figures were veiled by the darkness, no one else could identify the couple, but she was sure it was them. From his vantage point, the killer heard the couple enter Melanie's room—the faint sound of a struggle in a closed room.

Charlene leaned back on the bed and whispered, "That's why the door was unlocked... He was there before us. Oh, God, we let this happen..."

The video cut to the intruder standing in front of Melanie's door. He grabbed the door knob, then he barged into the room—completely disregarding the racket he caused. Melanie shrieked and crawled across the bed, terrified. The killer pulled a knife out of his pocket as he ran into the room.

Panting as she watched the tense video, Charlene whispered, "No, no, no. Please... I'm so sorry, Melanie."

Melanie stopped screaming. She gasped as the knife penetrated her stomach. Without hesitation, the cameraman pulled the knife out, then he stabbed her again and again. The blade sliced into her stomach and cut into her belly button—such a sensitive area. Gasping for air, Melanie kicked the killer's chest, which caused him to stumble back.

Melanie seized the opportunity and lurched out of the room. The cameraman followed closely behind. He crashed into the wall as he ran into the hallway. He chuckled upon spotting the shocked expression on the young woman's face.

Holding her hands over her stomach, Melanie shouted, "Mom! Mom, no!"

The cameraman turned his head and glanced into the living room. The footage depicted Melanie's mother.

The woman leaned back in her seat. A red tie was tightly wrapped around her neck. Her wrists were slit vertically. A brown bottle of beer was shoved into her mouth. The mouth of the bottle reached into her throat and her teeth scraped the body of the bottle. Blood dribbled down her chin. The crumbs of crushed sleeping pills sat on her lips, too. She was clearly forced to swallow a handful of sleeping pills before the beer bottle was shoved down her throat. She was viciously murdered.

Weeping uncontrollably, Melanie ran through the front door. As she ran onto the porch, the killer stabbed the small of her back. Melanie shrieked and stumbled down the porch steps. Yet, she continued to move forward. The resilient teenager lurched across the walkway and pushed herself through the gate.

As she landed on the police cruiser, Melanie shouted, "Help! Help me! He's here! He's–"

Watching the footage, Charlene asked, "What are you doing? Why aren't they helping you?"

As the killer reached the car, Charlene found the reason. The cop in the car was dead. His throat was slit from ear-to-ear. Blood cascaded down his neck and poured over his chest.

The cameraman grabbed a fistful of Melanie's hair, then he smashed her face through the passenger seat window. He pulled her head back, then he slammed her face on the side-view mirror. The mirror broke off of the car. Shards of glass were trapped in the grisly gashes on her face. Her torture was not over, though.

The killer continued slamming her face on the car door. A dull *clanging* sound echoed through the street with each hit. Blood streamed across the white door and plopped on the street. The masked person stopped after the fifteenth hit. He still held a fistful of Melanie's hair, but the woman did not move. Melanie died during the attack—and the killer didn't notice until after the fact.

The masked person leaned closer to Melanie's face, making sure he recorded every gruesome detail. Her nose was crushed *into* her head, practically wiped off of her face. Her eyes were swollen shut. Bumps formed across her face, too. She had a large gash on her brow and several cuts across her cheeks. Due to the blood, bumps, and cuts, she was unidentifiable.

The killer glanced up upon hearing men and women screaming—Melanie's neighbors were shouting at them. The teenager's body fell onto the floor as the killer ran off, breathing heavily as he sprinted down the sidewalk. The video abruptly ended.

Eyes welling with tears, Charlene held her hand over her gaping mouth as she stared at the screen. She was rendered speechless by the senseless violence and tormented by her guilt. *A second, a minute*—she needed time to recompose herself.

***

Charlene wiped the tears from her rosy cheeks as she wheezed and groaned. She took several deep breaths, trying her best to calm her jitters. Although her peers happily spread the video, she was unnerved by the graphic violence. She wasn't desensitized like most of society. She opened Skype on her laptop and called Adam.

As she waited, Charlene whispered, "Come on, Adam. Your phone is out of service, but that doesn't mean your computer doesn't work. Come on, answer the call."

The call connected. Adam lay in bed in a dark room, shirtless with his hair tousled. He looked as if he had just woken up. Judging from the sly smirk on his face, Charlene assumed he didn't know about Melanie's demise—or perhaps he enjoyed the video.

Adam said, "Good morning, babe. I didn't expect you to–"

"Invite Michael and Stephen to the chat," Charlene interrupted. "I'll call Britney and Dominique."

Adam sat up in bed and asked, "What is this about?"

"We have to talk about something. Call them. *Now.*"

Adam could see the determination and fear in his girlfriend's eyes—a contradicting blend of courage and cowardice. Although she tried to hide it, he could also see the tears in her puffy eyes. He nodded in agreement, then he called Stephen.

Britney joined the chat. She asked, "Charlene, did you see it?"

"See what?" Adam asked.

Charlene responded, "We'll get to that in a minute. Just call them."

"I did. Michael's not answering, though. He's probably asleep or he's still pissed about last night."

"Yeah, Dominique's not answering, either. Shit, I hope they're okay..."

Britney furrowed her brow and said, "Wait a second. What happened last night?"

Surrounded by smoke, Stephen joined the call. It was barely seven in the morning and the young dealer was already smoking. Despite the drugs flowing through his system, the junior remained competent and attentive—especially around Charlene.

Stephen asked, "What's going on? Should I, um, you know... stop smoking?"

Charlene said, "I just... I wanted to wait for Michael and Dominique, but they're not answering. We don't have time to waste, either. There's a problem."

Adam asked, "What happened, Charles?"

Charlene vacantly stared down at her keyboard. She stared at the screen and examined her friends. Adam was unusually attentive, Stephen was nonchalant, and Britney was calm despite knowing about the violent video. She couldn't admit it to her friends, but she was suspicious of all of them. *Anyone could be the killer,* she thought.

Britney said, "I'm guessing this is about the video."

"What video?" Stephen asked.

"You guys, Melanie died last night. I don't know if it was the same person who killed Anna and Tiffany, but... *she's dead.* The killer recorded all of it, too. It's trending on Facebook, Instagram, Twitter... It's probably all over the news by now."

Charlene said, "It doesn't matter where it's trending. Forget about all of that. The killer is still out there and he's still killing. We could be next. We have to find a way to stop him or... or to hide from him. We have to do something."

The group became quiet. The truth stung like alcohol on a fresh wound. A serial killer was terrorizing their community with no signs of slowing down. Although there was some collateral damage, he was only targeting students from their school, too. They were all potential targets, whether they liked it or not.

Breaking the silence, Stephen asked, "So, who do you think is the killer?"

Britney said, "The video was trending under '#ForCasey.' Isn't Casey that kid who killed himself last year? Or is that just a coincidence?"

"It's not a coincidence," Charlene responded. "Casey has something to do with it, but it might be all some sort of trick."

"What do you mean?"

"We spoke to Wilson last night because we linked the killer's mask to him. I recognized the style and I knew he was connected. Well, it turned out that Casey Marshall gave him masks that look like the killer's mask. It's obviously not Casey, though. His masks are part of this puzzle, but he might have nothing to do with this."

Adam asked, "What are you saying, Charles?"

Charlene shuffled on her bed, then she explained, "What if someone was using Casey's death as a diversion? Hmm? What if Wilson was the killer and he was actually using Casey's masks to throw everyone off? He fits the description of the killer, right? He knows where we live, right? His students are the ones dying, *right?* He's the perfect suspect."

"He doesn't have a motive, though," Stephen said. He wagged his pipe at the webcam and said, "Most killers have motives. Unless we're in some crappy 'home invasion' movie where they did it because 'we were home,' he *has* to have a motive, Charlene. It's one of the rules of good storytelling."

Wide-eyed, Charlene said, "He *does* have a motive, though. Listen, last night, Adam and I confronted Melanie and Wilson about all of this. When–"

"Wait a second," Britney interrupted. "Was that *you* in that video? You and Adam?"

Charlene sighed in disappointment. She said, "Yes. Yes, it was us. We got there after that creep entered her house and we left before he hurt her. We didn't even know he was there. That's not the point, though. Listen, when we went to Wilson's house, we found out that Dominique was the one dating Wilson this whole time. The rumors were true. They're a couple."

With the juicy gossip, Britney's suspicion of Charlene was whisked away. She gasped and held her hands over her mouth. She was more surprised by the gossip than Melanie's murder. Stephen chuckled and shook his head, amused by the news. He took another puff from his pipe.

Charlene continued, "So, maybe Wilson is killing the people who know about his relationship with Dominique. Maybe he's such a sick pervert that he's lost all control and he's going on a rampage. It's happened before, right? And, if it's happened before, it can happen again."

Again, the group became quiet. Adam stared deeply at his girlfriend, as if he were suspicious of her intentions. Stephen absently stared at a wall, lost in his thoughts. Britney sucked her lips inward and waited for the next word.

Adam said, "I don't think we can throw Wilson

under the bus yet. We need more evidence. We should find Hailey."

"Hailey?" Stephen repeated in an uncertain tone.

"Yeah, Hailey Washington. If that rumor was right, then she was there when Tiffany died. She's the only person we haven't confronted."

The teenagers nodded in agreement.

Britney said, "That sounds like a good plan, but does anyone know where she lives? I've seen her around school, we have a few classes together, but I've never spoken to her."

"I know where she lives," Stephen said. He took another puff, then he blew a cloud of smoke at his webcam. As the smoke cleared, the stoner said, "I've sold to her before. If we're going, I'm gonna need a ride."

Britney said, "If you can't get Michael, I can borrow my mom's car and pick you all up. Sound good?" *Yes, yeah*—the teenagers mumbled. Britney said, "Okay. I'll pick up Charlene first, then Adam, then Stephen. I'll see you guys in a few."

Britney waved, then she disconnected from the call. Stephen, coughing and grunting, indistinctly mumbled his goodbyes. Alone with his girlfriend, Adam stared at Charlene. He nodded at her, then he disconnected from the call.

Charlene closed her laptop, then she tossed the computer aside. She sat in silence on her bed, lost in a maze of doubt. She was suspicious of everyone.

Adam was quickly crossed off her list, though, since he was with her when they arrived at Melanie's house. Britney could have been the killer, but she didn't quite fit the description. From her group of friends, Stephen was the last person on her list.

She whispered, "Stephen, Stephen, Stephen... You know where everyone lives, don't you? I don't know what to think of you. I just hope it's not you."

She sighed in disappointment, then she started to prepare for her day.

Chapter Thirteen

Where's Hailey?

From the passenger seat of the SUV, Charlene glanced around the neighborhood. The houses were small, the parked cars were old, and the lawns were unkempt. The neighborhood was not as fortunate as hers. Still, the area was cozy and welcoming. There was a sense of community in the neighborhood.

She stared at a beige two-story house and asked, "So, this is Hailey's house? Are you sure?"

Sitting behind her, Stephen nodded and said, "Yeah. I've been here before. I haven't been inside 'cause she didn't want me to come in, but I've been here. She lives with her grandma, I think."

"Well, let's go see if Hailey will talk to us."

Charlene climbed out of the car, her friends following behind her. She walked past the chain-link fence, strolling up the walkway as she examined the front of the house. She didn't see anyone at the windows, though. Something was afoot, but she couldn't put her finger on it. Her mind was clouded with ominous thoughts.

Charlene knocked on the crimson-red door—*thud, thud, thud.* She clasped her hands behind her back as she patiently waited. She glanced back at her friends upon hearing a set of lumbering footsteps inside of the house.

The door swung open.

An elderly woman in a floral-print duster and

matching slippers stood in the doorway—*Louise Washington.* Louise squinted and adjusted her glasses as she stared at the teenagers. She didn't appear frightened or threatened by the group's presence. She smiled—the tender, heartwarming smile of a loving grandmother.

Louise said, "Oh, you must be Hailey's friends. How can I help you?"

Charlene responded, "Hello, Mrs. Washington. We were just hoping to speak to Hailey for a few minutes if that's okay. Is she home?"

"Of course, of course. I'm sure she wouldn't mind. Come in, make yourselves comfortable," Louise said as she beckoned to the teenagers. As she stepped aside, allowing the teenagers to enter her home, Louise said, "And, please, call me Louise. No need for the 'miss' or 'missus.' Okay?"

"Okay," the teenagers simultaneously responded.

Louise approached the stairs directly ahead of the front door. She knocked on the wall beside an archway to her right. The knocking echoed through the house.

Louise shouted, "Hailey, your little friends are here! Come down, sweetie!" There was no response. Smiling, she glanced back at the teenagers and said, "She's probably listening to music. Your music is so loud these days. I wouldn't be surprised if you lost your hearing before me."

She chuckled and shook her head, then she hit the wall again.

As Louise knocked, Charlene glanced around the home. The archway to her right led to the living room. Polaroid photographs were framed and pinned to the walls. The furniture was outdated—a tube television, a record player, and the gist—but it all seemed to work. Through the archway to her left, she could see the kitchen. The dishes were clean and the table was neat. The woman was old and absent, but she took care of herself well.

Charlene asked, "Is anyone else home? Or do you live alone with Hailey?"

Louise nodded and said, "We live alone. Ever since Hailey's older brother went off to college, we've been holding down the fort—as some would say."

"Her brother?" Stephen repeated in a doubtful tone. "You–You're talking about Anthony?"

"Yes. You know him? Such a sweet boy, isn't he?"

"Yeah... Yeah. I mean, he was cool."

The teenagers glanced at each other. They knew about Anthony. He didn't go to college. He passed away two years prior in a drunk driving accident. His promising career in sports and academics was cut short by a fool who drank too much and decided to drive. The friends decided not to remind her about her grandson's death.

Charlene asked, "Do you think it would be okay if we went up there to talk to her? We'll be fast and respectful, I promise."

Louise puckered her lips and shrugged. She said, "You seem like good kids... I suppose that's okay. I think Hailey would appreciate it. She's been acting a little strange lately. Go ahead. Her room is the first on the right." As the group walked up the stairs, the friendly woman asked, "Would you like me to bring up some tea and cookies? Or maybe some coffee?"

Charlene shouted, "No, thank you! We'll be fine!"

"Alrighty then! I'll be down here if you need anything. Have fun."

The group stopped at the top of the stairs and gazed at the first door on the right.

Charlene asked, "Do you think she'll try to fight us? Should we... Should we rush her?"

"*Rush her?*" Britney repeated, awed. "Jeez, Charles, she's not an animal. Let's just go in there and talk. If she doesn't want to, then we should just leave. It's as easy as that. I don't think Mrs. Washington needs anymore drama in her life. I definitely don't want her to see us holding her granddaughter down like that. I'm not going to jail over this."

"Fine. Let's just... talk to her. Come on," Charlene said. The group approached the door. As she knocked, Charlene said, "Hailey, it's Charlene. I had you in English last year, remember? We don't really talk, but I think we have Math together, too. Can we talk now?"

There was no response. The friends glanced over at each other, confused.

Charlene leaned closer to the door and said, "It's really important. I'm... I'm going to open the door, okay? I'm coming in." She glanced back at her friends as she reached for the door knob. She repeated, "I'm coming in..."

Hailey's bedroom was empty. The bed on the other side of the room was disheveled, the bed sheets rumpled and torn. The desk to the right was normal, but the computer chair was knocked over. A dime bag of weed sat atop the dresser to the right.

Crumbs of the marijuana were scattered across the dresser. And, most disconcerting of all, dried blood stained the floorboards towards the center of the room.

There was a struggle in the bedroom—and Hailey was nowhere to be found.

As she glanced around the room, eyes wide with fear, Britney asked, "What happened here?"

Adam tiptoed over the blood and approached the center of the room. He said, "We don't have a lot of options here, guys. We either run out of here and call the cops or..."

"Or what?" Stephen asked.

"*Or,* we seize the opportunity and take a look around. If we tell the cops, they'll lock this house down and they won't tell anyone about what they find. Personally, I think it would be best if we left all of this alone. But, I'm down if you're down. What do you want to do?"

The students glanced at each other, Adam had already voiced his opinion—he wanted to leave. Britney grimaced and shuddered, terrified. Stephen was stern and worried, but he would follow Charlene to the depths of hell if she asked.

Charlene said, "We'll take a quick look around, then we'll call the cops." She glanced over at Stephen, then at Britney. She said, "You guys can leave if you want. I don't want to drag you into any trouble."

Stephen responded, "I'll... I'll stick around. I sold weed to her, remember? If something happened, I need to know if it had anything to do with me."

Britney took a deep breath, then she said, "I can't

leave without you, Charlene. You know that. I'll wait here, but I'm not going to look around. I–I'm not going to get involved."

Charlene said, "Okay, that's fine. The rest of us will take a look. Let's just try not to touch anything."

***

Adam approached the bed. He tried to straighten the red bed sheets with his foot. He noticed the dark specks contrasting against the sheets—*blood.* The blood even stained the wooden frame of the bed and dripped down to the floor. He assumed the struggle started on her mattress. Just like Melanie, she was cut multiple times on her bed.

The young man knelt down at the foot of the bed, as if he were about to pray before going to sleep. He checked under the bed—nothing out of the ordinary.

Adam said, "She was probably stabbed over here. You know, she was probably texting or calling someone when the bastard crept up behind her and shanked her."

As he examined the nugget of weed on the dresser, Stephen said, "She was probably smoking. She was high when she was attacked."

"Yeah? How do you know that?"

"I'm not 100-percent positive, but it just looks like it. I sold her two dime-bags a few days ago and there's only one here. Her pipe is missing, too. So, she probably packed a bowl, laid up in bed, and smoked her shit."

Charlene nodded and said, "I think you're right. The killer stabbed her on the bed. Hailey put up a fight and wrestled with him. She tried to run, but he just pulled her back. She bumped into the chair, knocked it over, then she fell down here. He stabbed her until she died."

Stephen said, "Yeah, that works. But, where's the pipe?"

Adam asked, "No, man, *where's the body?*"

The teenagers glanced at each other, thinking about the clues and the questions. Two significant pieces of evidence were missing from the crime scene. They would have loved to find her phone, but the body and the pipe were known variables in the equation—they needed them to find the solution.

Britney pointed at the floor and said, "*Look.* The blood, it leads to the... the closet."

Indeed, a trail of blood led to the closet to Charlene's left. Charlene glanced at her friends and nodded, communicating without uttering a word— *I'm opening it.* With a trembling hand, she pulled the door open. Charlene and Britney gasped and staggered while Adam and Stephen gaped at the closet—wide mouths and bulging eyes.

As the door swung open, Hailey's body fell forward and landed face-first in front of the closet. As speculated, the teenage girl's torso was riddled with stab wounds. At the small of her back, her white shirt was soaked in blood. Her palms were also sliced, as if she had grabbed the killer's blade in order to stop the attack. The pipe was nowhere in sight, though.

Wheezing as if she were out of breath, Britney stuttered, "Th–That's... That's Hailey. Oh, God. Sh–She's dead. He killed her!"

Adam sternly said, "Keep your voice down. It won't look good if we get caught with a dead body here."

"What? Are you... Are you fucking kidding me right now? *She's dead.* There's a dead body right in front of us!"

Eyes full of tears, Charlene grabbed Britney's wrists and turned her away from the bloody sight. She gazed into Britney's bloodshot eyes. Again, she communicated without uttering a sound—*it's okay, I'm here.* She even caressed her cheek, trying to reassure her with her gentle touch.

Britney shook her head and mumbled indistinctly, unable to control herself. She fell into Charlene's arms and buried her face in her friend's chest as she sobbed.

Charlene glanced over at Adam and asked, "What do we do now?"

Adam shrugged—*I don't know.*

Stephen took a deep breath, then he said, "The pipe. Um... We have to find the pipe."

Charlene responded, "The pipe isn't important. We have to call the police. We have to tell–" She stopped as Stephen approached the body. She asked, "What are you doing?"

Stephen grimaced as he shoved his foot under Hailey's arm. He tried to lift his foot, but she was too heavy. So, Adam shoved his foot under her thigh and helped. Together, the young men lifted their legs and carefully flipped Hailey onto her back. The group shared a gasp of shock and disgust.

Charlene held Britney's face closer to her chest and said, "Don't look. Whatever you do, *don't look.*"

Hailey's face was horribly mutilated. Her cheeks and lips were swollen and bruised. Her nose was crushed, reduced to a bloody nub. Her left eye was swollen. Her right eye, however, suffered the most. Her glass marijuana pipe was shoved into her right eye socket. The bowl was still packed, so it was hot when the killer thrust it into her eye socket.

It appeared as if the killer tried to use the pipe as a makeshift spoon to scoop her eye out. He failed in removing her eye, but he was able to crush it.

As he held his shirt over his mouth, Stephen gagged and stuttered, "Th–There's... There's something in her... her mouth."

"Grab it," Adam directed, covering his mouth with his hand. Stephen glanced over at him with wide eyes—*are you serious?* Adam nodded and said, "Just cover your hand with your shirt and pull it out. I think it's a note."

Stephen stared at Adam with a deadpan expression, then he glanced over at Charlene. He could see it in her eyes: she wanted him to reach into Hailey's mouth, too. He sighed in disappointment, then he covered his hand with his shirt. He grabbed the crumpled sheet of paper from the victim's mouth, then he shook his hand to unwrap the note.

"What does it say?" Charlene asked.

Stephen responded, "It's a... a hashtag. It says: *#ForCasey.*"

Adam asked, "Casey? Like, Casey Marshall? Does... Does that mean..."

"It means he recorded it," Charlene said as she vacantly stared at the ceiling. "Yeah. He recorded it and he uploaded it with that hashtag. He did the same thing with Melanie. He probably did the same thing with the others, too."

Aside from Britney's hysterical bawling—she could still hear the entire conversation after all—the group became quiet. They were stunned by the revelation. They could only wonder if the killer's rampage was over or if they were targets of his lust for blood.

Upon feeling the vibrations on her leg, Charlene pulled her cell phone out of her pocket. She swiped the tears from her eyes and stared at the screen.

As she put the phone on speaker, she said, "It's Dominique." She answered, "Dominique, we've been trying to call you all morning. Wh–Where are you? We... We have some bad news."

Sniveling, Dominique said, "Charles, he's dead. He's really dead."

"What? What are you talking about? Who's dead?"

"M–Michael. They... They found his body over home-plate at the Kamala baseball field."

Charlene took several deep breaths as she absorbed the information. *If Michael is dead,* she thought, *the killer wasn't only after Tiffany and her friends.* She could see the fear in all of her friends' eyes, but she remained strong.

As a tear streamed down her cheek, Charlene asked, "Are you at the field right now?"

"Y–Yes. There's a huge crowd out here. Police, paramedics, news reporters... Everyone is out here."

"We're going to be right there, okay? Wait for us in the parking lot."

"O–Okay, Charlene. Please, come as fast as possible. I don't want to be here all alone. This is... This is just so scary."

Charlene said, "I'll be there in a minute. Stay strong, sweetie."

She hung up the phone and stared at her friends, waiting for someone to take command. To her dismay, her friends remained quiet. Their eyes wandered around the room, refusing to look down at Hailey.

Charlene coughed to clear her throat, then she said, "You all heard it: Michael is dead. That means we're in trouble, too. We can't stand around here and wait to die, though. We need to start moving."

Stephen asked, "So, what do we do now?"

"We're going to do exactly as I say. Two of us will go meet with Dominique at the baseball field and the other two will stay here and deal with... *this*."

Puffy-eyed, Britney shook her head and said, "Charlene, we can't tell her grandmother about this. It would break her heart. I... I can't hurt her like that. Damn it, why is this happening to us? What did we do to deserve this?"

Charlene responded, "Okay. Whoever stays won't have to tell her. Just call the cops anonymously and tell them everything. Wait until they arrive, then leave and meet us at Big's Burgers in an hour. Okay?" The teenagers nodded in agreement—*okay*. Charlene asked, "So, who's staying and who's going?"

Britney said, "I'll stay. I don't want to see Michael like that. I don't want to see anymore dead bodies."

Stephen said, "I can't stay. I've got some bud on me. I don't... I don't want to get caught around here. I know it, they'll link all of this to me just 'cause I sold her some weed. I'm going."

"Then I'll stay," Adam said. "Dominique called you,

Charles, so she expects to see you. I'll stick around here."

Britney asked, "If that's how it's going to be, do you guys need a ride or something?"

Charlene responded, "No. The field is just a few blocks down. We can jog over there, then we can walk to Big's. Just call me if anything happens." She beckoned to Stephen and said, "Let's hurry."

The friends said their goodbyes. Charlene and Stephen crept out of the house, slinking past Louise in the living room, while Adam and Britney called the police from Hailey's bedroom.

Chapter Fourteen

Death Looming Over The City

Breathing heavily, Charlene and Stephen slowed from a jog to a stroll upon reaching the baseball field. The field was cordoned off by the police—detectives discussed the case near the foul lines while forensic specialists combed the area for evidence. Michael lay on top of home-plate. His body was not covered yet in order to preserve the crime scene.

As she approached Dominique, Charlene frowned and said, "I'm sorry. I'm so sorry."

Dominique grimaced and sobbed, then she fell into Charlene's arms and cried into her chest. She released all of the sorrow in her system, mourning the death of a special friend.

Teary-eyed, Charlene patted the back of Dominique's head and said, "I don't know what to say. I know you were having problems, but... Shit, this is just too much. It's fucked up."

In a muffled tone, Dominique asked, "Why would someone do this to him? Why... Why is that bastard killing us?"

"I don't know, sweetie, I just don't know. I don't think he's going to stop any time soon, though. We're all in trouble."

Dominique pulled away from Charlene's embrace. She stared at her close friend with a furrowed brow, rattled by the ominous statement.

She asked, "What are you talking about? How do you know he's not done? How do you know we... we're in trouble?"

Chiming in, Stephen said, "He killed Melanie and Hailey, and now your boyfriend is dead. We're fucked, Dom. Obviously, these pigs aren't doing their jobs. We should have gone to Vegas when we had the chance... *Fuck.*"

Dominique was shocked by the news, rendered speechless by the blunt truth. She glanced at Charlene, hoping to receive some sensible words of reassurance, but her friend remained silent. She grimaced and sobbed again, crippled by her fear.

As she stared at the field, Charlene said, "I don't know what to do... I'm out of ideas. Damn it, I just don't know what to do anymore."

"What are you kids doing here?" a gruff voice asked from behind the group.

The students turned towards the voice. Sheriff Cameron Jackson approached from behind them. The man walked with two other officers. He beckoned to the officers and motioned his demands —*go to the field, don't let anyone through, you know the drill.*

He stopped beside the students and said, "You should be home right now. You shouldn't be roaming the streets."

The students, despondent and quiet, stared down at their feet. Their shame and fear could be seen from a mile away. Charlene, in particular, was worried Jackson would recognize her from Melanie's footage. *It was dark,* she thought, *he couldn't recognize me, it's impossible.*

Jackson sighed, then he asked, "Did you see anything over here?" The students glanced up at him, curious. Jackson clarified, "Did any of you know the victim?"

Before Dominique could respond, Charlene said, "We saw him around school. He was a... a friend. We wouldn't know anything else about him, so don't bother asking."

She gave a hostile response in order to stop Jackson from taking them to the station. The police weren't able to protect the students throughout the past week, so she didn't trust him. At the back of her mind, she even believed a police officer could be responsible. *He could tamper with the evidence,* she thought, *there's no way they're that incompetent.*

Jackson said, "Okay, okay. I just want you to know: every detail helps. If you knew the victim, if you knew if he was in any trouble with any rough crowds, it would help us bring justice to these streets if you told us about it."

"Rough crowds?" Dominique repeated in disbelief. "What? Do you think this was gang-related? I saw him when I got here. He looked like he was attacked by an animal! He was slaughtered, just like our other classmates!"

Unable to contain herself, Charlene jabbed her finger at the officer's chest and said, "You were supposed to protect us. You said no one else would get hurt!"

Jackson sighed in disappointment. He felt guilty for his perceived failures. He was trying to catch a serial killer while keeping the situation under control. The bodies were quickly piling up, though, and hell was breaking loose in the city.

Jackson said, "I won't force you into anything, I don't have the right to do that, but I'd really appreciate it if you came down to the station with me. We can talk about this. We can help you and you can help us."

Stephen said, "No, no, no. That's what you always say. 'We're just putting you in handcuffs, you're not under arrest,' but you always arrest them. If we go with you, we'd just be cornering ourselves, and if you're the kill–" He stopped himself from making the baseless claim. He said, "It's... It's just not worth it. We don't know anything anyway."

Charlene said, "Stephen's right. We can't trust anyone. I mean, we can barely trust ourselves, so how could we trust you? We don't know why you haven't caught the guy, we don't know where you've been. I can't do it, I can't go..."

Jackson said, "Like I told you: I'm not going to force you into the back of a police car. I can't do that to you. Not after all of this... I want you to be safe, though. You need to trust us just like I'm trusting you to do the right thing." He sighed as he glanced over at the field, dismayed by the tragedy. He said, "Listen, if you won't come with me, I think it would be best if you went home—*together*. Pick one house where you know your parents will be home, lock all of the doors, then have a... a sleepover or something. If you can't do that, stay at your own houses and lock yourselves in. Whatever you do, don't come out at night like this young man did. I don't want you running around these streets looking for trouble."

As she swiped at the tears clinging to her eyelids,

Charlene nodded and stuttered, "I–I... I think we can do that. S–Sure."

"Thank you. I want you to know: we're trying our best out here. There will be a mandatory curfew for the rest of the week, we're working directly with our neighborhood watch groups to keep a lookout over our communities 24/7, and the investigation is... it's moving, okay? We have some suspects who we'll be hauling in soon. We're making progress."

The students didn't have anything else to say to the sheriff. They simply nodded at him—*okay.* The sheriff returned the nod, then he moseyed towards the baseball field. He had to push through the concerned civilians and drama-starved reporters.

Dominique asked, "What's the plan, Charlene?"

As she stared at Michael's body from afar, Charlene said, "This isn't the place to talk... Adam and Britney are meeting us at Big's Burgers. Come on, I'll fill you in on the way."

As the group wandered away from the crime scene, Dominique glanced back at the field and whispered, "I'm sorry, Michael. I'm sorry for everything..."

***

Charlene, Dominique, and Stephen sat at a table outside of Big's Burgers, resting in the shade of a large umbrella. The world around them moved at the same pace as the day before—and it would surely move at the same pace during the next day. Some parents were concerned about their kids' well-being, especially with the fear-mongering media attempting to terrify everyone simply to retain viewership.

However, the chance of being killed by a serial killer was a fraction of one-percent, so it didn't really bother them. News programs served as entertainment and statistics made people feel better.

Adam and Britney approached the table.

Adam said, "We called the cops and waited across the street until they showed up. I think they found her body and I don't think Mrs. Washington saw us leave." He nodded at Charlene and asked, "How'd it go at the baseball field?"

Dominique scowled at Adam and responded, "How do you think it went? Huh? Didn't you hear? Michael is *dead.* He's gone. You fucking asshole..."

"I know, I know. I didn't mean to... to offend you. I was just asking in case anything else happened," Adam responded. He rubbed Dominique's shoulder and said, "I'm sorry. He was my friend, too. I don't... Shit, I don't know what else to say."

The group became quiet, taking a moment of silence to honor their slain friend. Although customers happily chattered around them, the atmosphere at the table was poignant—a black cloud poured a rain of pessimism over the friends.

Breaking the silence, Britney asked, "What are we going to do? I mean, we can't trust anyone, right? So, what do we do?"

Charlene said, "When we bumped into Sheriff Jackson at the field, he told us that we should all stick together and try to sleep at one house. It sounds like it could work, but... I don't know. What do you think?"

Stephen shook his head and said, "It's a stupid idea. It's not safe, either. I mean, just think about how easy it is to break into a house these days. Shit, it's even been done in movies. You've watched *Scream,* right? They all go to a house party at the end of the movie and, spoiler alert, people *still* end up dying. We can invite everyone to one of our houses and it wouldn't matter... Numbers don't mean shit in a horror movie."

Dominique said, "We're not in a damn horror movie or some true crime book. No one is sitting in their beds reading about this before they sleep."

"Movie, book, reality... It doesn't matter. The same rules apply. It's not safe."

Adam said, "But, it would be five against one. We would be able to take care of ourselves either way, right?"

Charlene vacantly stared at the table. She thought about horror movies and books. Although her favorite movies were works of fiction, she believed most movies were based on real life. Therefore, fictional scenarios could help her survive. Violent media was not as 'worthless' as some pseudo-intellectuals would argue.

Charlene said, "In *Scream,* there was more than one killer... What if it's the same here? What if this killer isn't working alone?"

Adam huffed, then he responded, "The same twist? That would just be lazy, Charles."

Dominique gritted her teeth as she grabbed a fistful of her hair. The conversation was obnoxious. Her former boyfriend was dead. She was devastated by his unexpected demise. However, she was more concerned about her own safety. *Movies can't save us,* she thought.

Dominique said, "I can't believe this... What if it's like that kid that drowned in the lake? Huh? What if Jason *fucking* Voorhees is after us? What if Charlene's long-lost brother is back to celebrate Thanksgiving or 'French Toast Day?' What then?" She nervously chuckled and shook her head, flustered. She said, "This isn't a movie. Okay? Look, the sheriff said they're close to catching the guy. So, we either stick together and try to fight him off until they catch him or we split up. As far as I know, he doesn't have my number, Britney's number, or Adam's number. Splitting up might be better if we don't want Charlene and Stephen to get everyone killed... like Michael."

"What?" Charlene asked, sneering in disbelief. "Are you really blaming us for Michael's death?"

"You brought Michael along with you last night. You brought him out, you got him killed. None of this would have happened if it wasn't for you."

"You... You bitch. He would have never left us if you weren't cheating, you–"

"*Stop,*" Britney interrupted. She stopped the argument from snowballing out of control. She said, "I think you're both right. He's following us somehow. Maybe it is Charlene and Stephen, maybe it isn't. All we know is: everyone who died, they died alone. I think it would be best if we stuck together. We just have to find a place the killer wouldn't search. Not a house, not a park... We have to find somewhere that would be empty but... but secure at night."

Yet again, the group became quiet. Without uttering a word, they cycled through their options.

Houses were out of the questions—too many deaths occurred at home. Public spaces were also dangerous—the killer could be lurking anywhere. The police station seemed like the safest bet, but doubts still lingered in their minds.

Dominique said, "I have an idea." All of the students glanced at her, curious. Dominique said, "There's one place that's always empty and secure at night: *the school.* I can call Wilson and I can get him to sneak us into the school when the sun goes down. We'll go into one classroom and we'll wait until morning. The school is like a fortress and no one would ever think of us being there. And, the police station is, like, four or five blocks away. It's safe."

"Yeah. That can work," Charlene said. She glanced at the rest of the group and asked, "What do you think?"

The students glanced at each other, nervous and uncertain. They didn't have any better suggestions, though. Adam, Britney, and Stephen nodded in agreement.

Charlene turned towards Dominique and said, "Call him. See if you can convince him. Try to get him to stay with us, too. Everyone who knows we'll be there *has* to be there. Go ahead, call him."

Chapter Fifteen

The Last Stand

Two vehicles—Wilson's sedan and Britney's SUV—rolled to a stop at the side of the school, solely illuminated by the moonlight. Charlene, Adam, and Dominique rode with Wilson while Britney and Stephen rode in the SUV. The group arrived at their destination, but they didn't immediately exit their vehicles. They sat and stared at the empty school, as if they were uncertain of their plans.

Charlene asked, "Won't there be any security guards or janitors around?"

As he stared at the building, the fear of destroying his career sitting on his shoulders, Wilson responded, "No. The police are out with the Neighborhood Watch. They're patrolling the communities."

"And, what about the janitors?"

"Only one janitor works around here at night. I had to call him to borrow his keys. He doesn't know about all of... *this*. Besides, his shift is over now. I'm sure of it."

The interior of the car became silent. Charlene felt like she should have been asking more questions, but she couldn't say another word. Adam grabbed his girlfriend's hand and nodded at her—*everything's going to be okay*. Dominique kept her eyes locked on the building, anxious.

Wilson asked, "Are you sure you want to do this?"

Charlene said, "Yeah. I think it's our best option. For tonight, at least."

"We have an agreement, right? You'll keep quiet about... about us, and I'll help you this *one* time. There's no turning back on that, even if you get caught, okay?"

Charlene and Adam nodded—*okay.* Wilson turned towards his teenage lover. Dominique gave off half-a-smile and nodded in agreement.

Wilson said, "Alright. Let's get in there before someone sees us."

The group climbed out of the sedan. As they followed Wilson's lead, Charlene turned and beckoned to the couple in the SUV. Britney and Stephen glanced at each other—a glance of uncertainty—then they followed their friends. They examined the building as they strolled towards the front of the school.

The campus was clean and modern, but it still felt eerie. Schools always felt spooky when they were explored at night without any crowds.

Wilson turned the key, then he pushed the front doors open. The group stared down the dark, lonely hall—doubtful, nervous, frightened.

Wilson said, "We'll go to my classroom and none of you will leave my sight until we all decide to go home. Understood?"

Charlene glanced at her friends, then at Wilson. She said, "*Understood.*"

"Good. Come on. Try not to touch anything, either."

As Wilson closed the door behind them, the group slowly walked past the administration area to their right. They were afraid the principal might have been lurking around the campus—he was nowhere in sight, though. So, the group quietly walked past the first intersection and strolled down the locker-lined hallway.

Wilson's classroom was the fifth room to the right in the same corridor as the school's main entrance.

Wilson unlocked the door and said, "I think we should leave the lights off. We're not supposed to be here—*obviously.*"

He used an app on his cellphone to use his camera's flash as a light. From the whiteboard at the front of the class, he illuminated the rest of the room. To his relief, the coast was clear. A killer wasn't hiding under the desks or in the dimmest corners of the room.

As he sat on the rolling chair at his desk, the teacher said, "Maybe you guys should just sit near the front. You don't have to sit in your regular seats or anything like that." He nodded at Stephen and said, "I don't think I've ever even had you in a Math class."

Stephen said, "Yeah, you're right." He grabbed a desk from the front row and dragged it towards the whiteboard, then he spun it around. He said, "Well, I hope you don't mind if I move this. If you guys are going to sit in the front and look this way, someone should be looking at the back of the class. Someone other than this guy..."

As she took a seat at the front of the class, Charlene said, "Good thinking. We can keep an eye on the door while you watch our backs."

Dominique, Britney, and Adam sat at the other

desks in the front row. The group was silent. Stephen turned on the light on his phone and illuminated his friends. Charlene stared at the clock above the whiteboard, anxiously waiting for the night to end. Adam sat beside her, constantly glancing every which way—as if he were afraid of something. Britney scrolled through the social media apps on her phone, trying to keep her mind off of the mayhem.

Breaking the silence, Dominique gently laughed, then she said, "You know, I was so scared about all of this, I completely forgot to tell my parents about... *everything.* I mean, I didn't tell them anything at all. I didn't tell them where I was going or why. No excuses... I wonder if they're calling the cops."

Britney said, "Yeah, I did the same. My mom's been asking about her car all day. She's obviously worried, but I've just been trying to buy time. I've been ignoring her... Maybe it would be better if they called the cops. We could get arrested for trespassing and end up at the police station."

"Yeah, or we could have just gone with Sheriff Jackson a few hours ago. I know we shouldn't trust anyone, but it's not like he would have killed us at the station."

Stephen said, "If we went with that pig, I would have been arrested for sure." Wilson and the students glanced at him with curious eyes. Stephen cracked a smile and clarified, "For the weed. I'm not walking around with a quarter or all that, but they'll arrest you for anything these days."

The group shared a sigh of relief.

For a second, Charlene believed Stephen had

something to do with the murders. She didn't want to suspect him, but she was desperately searching for a suspect. Despite her fear of death, she would feel comfortable at least knowing the identity of the killer. The paranoia in her mind—the constant doubt picking at her brain—was driving her insane.

Adam said, "I still think we did the right thing. If we went to the police, they would have told our parents about everything, then our parents wouldn't let us see each other."

Britney said, "Yeah, I guess you're right. Adults are useless in horror movies, aren't they?"

Dominique smirked and glanced over at Wilson. She said, "You hear that, sweetie? You're useless."

Wilson bit his bottom lip and nodded, disregarding the playful insult. He wasn't concerned about the students and their discussion. He was solely worried about being caught at the school with his teenage students. It didn't paint a pretty picture.

Charlene leaned forward on her desk and said, "Instead of just sitting here until morning, maybe we should talk about all of this."

"About what?" Stephen asked. "We already talked about leaving and telling the cops, and we just got here. What are we going to talk about?"

"The murders. I've been thinking about it all day, trying to link the deaths to someone, but I just can't think of anyone. There's only one common denominator: *Casey's masks.* Do you guys remember Casey and his family?"

"I sold weed to Casey's brother once—Nico. Nico Marshall. He seemed like a good dude. They kind of disappeared after Casey... *you know.* It died down really quick, too. The kid died and everyone forgot about it in, like, a week. It's sad shit."

Britney nodded and said, "Yeah. He had a younger sister, too—Bethany. He was one grade below her. Or was it the other way around?" She smiled—a bittersweet smile. She said, "I remember seeing Beth and Casey in the cafeteria. They'd always eat lunch together. Some kids made fun of them for that, but I thought it was cute. Brothers and sisters should take care of each other..."

Charlene said, "Well, maybe it's not a cop, a teacher, or a parent... Maybe this is a vengeance thing. Casey committed suicide because he was being bullied. What if someone is trying to avenge him?"

The group sat in silence as they considered the tragic possibility.

Charlene continued, "I don't think it can be Bethany. She was... She was just soft, you know? She wouldn't be capable of doing... *that* to anyone. And, besides, Melanie said the killer was big—big enough to be a teacher."

Britney said, "If that's all true, then it might be Nico. I mean, I don't really remember what he looks like, but it makes sense. So... has anyone seen Nico recently?"

Yet again, the students remained quiet. While the teenagers stared at their desks, clearly contemplating the question, Wilson carefully examined the students. In the dark, barely illuminated by a cell phone's light, he had trouble reading them. He sucked his lips inward and nodded. He didn't want to get involved, but he had information—and the pieces were starting to come together.

Wilson said, "Last year in my math class, before Casey passed away, I vividly remember you, *Adam,* were a good friend of Nico's. I'm pretty sure I sent you and Nico to detention together a few times. Isn't that right?"

Adam furrowed his brow as he stared at his teacher. The expression on his face read: *what the hell are you doing?* He was thrown under the bus by a man who was supposed to protect him. He glanced at his friends—they all stared back at him with narrowed eyes.

Adam stuttered, "I–I don't... I don't know what you're thinking, but–"

"Did you kill Michael?" Dominique interrupted, furious.

"Wha–What? Are... Are you kidding me? How could you say that? He was, like, my... my best friend."

Britney said, "You've been distant lately. You haven't been answering Charlene's calls. You were late the day after Tiffany died. You disappear and reappear whenever you want... It adds up, doesn't it?"

Adam nervously chuckled, then he said, "I didn't kill anyone. I mean, just think about what you're saying. I was with most of you the night Michael died." He turned towards Charlene and said, "I was with *you* when we went to go talk to Melanie because *you* wanted us to."

Charlene nodded and said, "He's right. In Melanie's video, it shows both of us going into

Melanie's house. There was someone else there."

Through the darkness, Charlene gazed into her boyfriend's eyes—*you're not the killer, are you?* Adam returned the gaze, trying to convince his girlfriend with a set of glimmering puppy eyes— *please, believe me.*

Britney said, "I don't think it matters if you *physically* did it. You're still the most suspicious person here. I mean, you... you could have been working with the real killer! Nico could have been killing everyone with your help. Oh, God, did you–"

Frustrated, Dominique slapped her desk with both of her palms. The *thud* echoed through the classroom and seeped into the lonely halls.

She said, "I think you should leave, Adam. Right, guys? If he's the lead suspect, we should lock him out and spend the rest of the night here. *Right?*" Her peers weren't as quick to toss their friend out, though. Dominique huffed, then she said, "Either he leaves or I do."

"It's *not* me," Adam sternly said. "I don't think it was Nico, either. You keep saying he was as big as a teacher, as big as Wilson, but Nico wasn't that tall."

Chiming-in, Charlene glanced over at Dominique and said, "Think about what you're saying. If Adam is the killer or an accomplice, then it would be best if he stayed in our sight, right? He can't overpower all of us. We should just stick to the plan."

"Yeah, you're right," Stephen said as he leaned forward in his desk, elbows on the tabletop.

Dominique stared at her friends in disbelief. They spoke about the potential killers, they found evidence against Adam, but they refused to throw him out. She couldn't tell if they were naive, stupid, or brilliant. Their plan seemed logical on the surface, but she felt like it would crumble at the first sign of trouble.

Dominique glared at Wilson and said, "I need the keys for the restroom. I have to pee and I... I just need some air. I can't be around all of you."

Wilson said, "We had an agreement. You're not supposed to leave my sight. I just don't think that's a good idea."

"Just give me the keys, Wilson. I'm not in the mood for this."

Wilson sighed and pulled the keys out of his pocket, obedient like a trained dog. He said, "Fine. I don't want you to go alone and I want you back here in ten minutes."

Charlene said, "Stephen, you should go with her."

Stephen furrowed his brow and asked, "What? Why?"

"She should be with someone who can protect her and you're the only guy I trust right now."

"Fine," Stephen responded. He glanced at Dominique and said, "*Ten minutes.*"

Dominique said, "Whatever. Let's go."

As Dominique and Stephen departed, Charlene glanced around the room. Wilson sat with his legs up on his desk, trying to keep a semblance of control. Britney sat to her right, flicking her finger across her cell phone screen. Adam sat beside Charlene. His arms were hidden under his desk—she recognized his position.

Charlene asked, "Are you texting, Adam?"

Adam glanced up, surprised. He stuttered, "N–

No."

"What are you doing with your phone? I thought you didn't have service?"

"I don't. I was just going to play some music. Just 'cause I don't have service that doesn't mean the phone doesn't work. Damn, get off my back."

Charlene stared at Adam as he continued tinkering with his phone. She was suspicious, fear burdened her mind, but she couldn't muster the courage to confront him. With Stephen and Dominique gone, their numbers dwindled—and their chances of survival consequently decreased. She kept her eyes locked on Adam, though, ready to defend herself at a moment's notice.

Chapter Sixteen

Bathroom Break

Dominique stopped in front of the girls' restroom. She spun around and stared at her personal guard. Stephen followed closely behind her, using his cell phone to illuminate their path. He hopped and cocked his head back, surprised by his friend's sudden stop.

Stephen asked, "Aren't you, you know, going to handle your business?"

Dominique puckered her lips and nodded. She said, "Yeah, I'm going to get to that. I have to talk to you about something first."

She playfully twirled her hair as she stepped closer to Stephen. As if the young man used a marijuana-scented cologne, she could smell the weed on him. It didn't bother her, though. She was a smoker, too.

Her body pressed on his, Dominique softly said, "I need your help, Stephen. I think we both know Adam had something to do with all of those deaths. The others won't listen to me 'cause they're all afraid of being 'bad' friends. I need you to be on my side, then Britney will follow, then Wilson... then Charlene. After that, we can get rid of Adam and survive the night. Please, help me."

Stephen shook his head and stuttered, "I–I don't know about that. He... He's our friend."

"*Please,* Stephen," Dominique said in an unusually

honeyed voice. She ran her fingers across his crotch, teasing him. She said, "You do me a favor and I'll do you a favor. Okay? You scratch my back and I'll... I'll massage *something* for you. I'll massage it with my hands, my body... *my tongue.*"

Stephen grabbed Dominique's wrist and pushed her hand away from him. He shook his head as he stepped in reverse. His heart belonged to one girl. His unrequited love appeared hopeless, but he was willing to do anything for Charlene.

Dominique sneered in disgust and said, "You're such a spineless bitch, Stephen." As she strutted into the restroom, she said, "Wait out here and don't bother me, you selfish bastard."

As the door closed, Stephen turned around and muttered, "Whatever. You can't even go to the bathroom by yourself, bitch..."

Dominique sat on the toilet in the first stall. The sound of pee splashing in the toilet echoed through the quiet room. As she urinated, she furrowed her brow and peered through the crack on the door. She heard a peculiar sound—*creak.* She thought: *a squeaky hinge?* The sound of a few drops of piss plopping in the water reverberated through the room as she nearly finished urinating.

Just a few more drops.

Dominique gasped and hopped in her seat. She held her hand over her gaping mouth as she stared at the wall to her right, eyes wide with fear. Over the *plopping* sounds, she swore she heard a light footstep—quickly followed by another. The restroom door was to her left, though. There were four other stalls and a set of small windows to her right.

Was someone in here before I got here?–she thought.

As her breathing intensified, Dominique shouted, "Stephen! Stephen, is that you?"

There was no response. The deafening silence was unnerving. Although she feared the killer, she just wanted to hear something—*anything*—in the restroom.

Teary-eyed, Dominique said, "Stephen, you better not be peeping, you freakin' perv. Please, don't... don't hurt me. I was just–"

The hinges squealed as the restroom door swung open.

From the hallway, Stephen poked his head into the restroom and asked, "Is everything okay in here, Dom? I thought I heard you shout."

Dominique sniffled as she wiped the tears from her eyes. She shouted, "I'm fine. I'll be out in a minute."

"Alright, just hurry up. It's kinda creepy out here in the dark..."

"Yeah, sure..."

Dominique whimpered as the door closed. She wanted to cry for help, she thought about begging Stephen to stay inside with her, but she couldn't muster the courage to ask. Her inflated ego wouldn't allow her to ask for a helping hand. She wiped herself, then she let the neatly folded toilet paper fall into the water.

With the toilet flushing behind her, Dominique approached the sinks. She carefully examined her reflection as she washed her hands—as if she didn't recognize herself. She grimaced and whimpered, breaking down due to the stress and fear burdening her timid shoulders. Her legs wobbled, her hands trembled, and her shoulders shuddered.

Before she could fall to her knees and weep, the door of the stall in the center swung open.

Through the reflection on the mirror, Dominique could see her uninvited guest. At that moment, time froze. The water stopped splashing, the stall door stopped rattling, and the lights stopped buzzing. The couple locked eyes through the reflection on the mirror.

Once again, the killer wore a black raincoat with a hood, dark jeans, and steel-toe boots. His face was veiled by a paper-mâché joker mask. The mask was decorated with clown makeup—smeared lipstick, vibrant eye-shadow, wide-arching eyebrows, and a red nose. Bloody tears were painted across the cheeks, too.

As time continued at its regular pace, Dominique glanced down at the intruder's hands. He held a large pair of garden shears. The sharp blades sent chills down her spine. A quavering breath escaped her pale lips.

She turned towards the door and screamed, "He's here!"

As she took her first step towards the door, the killer lunged towards her with the shears wide open. Dominique shrieked and staggered down to her knees as the blades penetrated the small of her back —*around* her spine. The intruder kicked her shoulder, causing the girl to fall to her stomach. The cheerleader tried to squirm forward, but to no avail.

The killer's boot was firmly planted on her shoulder, pinning her to the ground.

The killer gritted his teeth as he tried to push the handles of the shears closer together—while the blades were still jammed into her flesh. Despite Dominique's resistance, squirming and shrieking, the masked person continued to open and close the shears until he reached her spine. A soft chuckle surfaced from behind the mask as the sound of Dominique's flesh *squishing* and her spine *crunching* emerged.

Stephen pushed the door open and stared into the restroom, awed. He saw the killer on top of Dominique, opening and closing the shears as he ripped through her spine. He saw Dominique on the floor, wheezing and groaning as she weakly reached for the door. She was paralyzed from the waist-down, though. A puddle of dark blood formed under her stomach.

Stephen stuttered, "Wha–What... What are you doing? What... What the *fuck* are you doing to her?!"

The attacker glanced up at Stephen. The stoner and killer gazed at each other. The masked person did not appear alarmed. In fact, he continued pushing on the shears' handles as he stared at Stephen. Stephen was surprised, though. The killer appeared smaller than he expected—smaller than him, in fact. He recognized something in the killer's eyes, too.

Stephen shook his head and snapped out of his trance, then he rushed into the room. He stepped over Dominique's body. He slid on her blood, but he was able to keep his footing. He pushed the killer off of her, causing him to stagger in reverse. He didn't have time to drag Dominique out of the room, so he decided to put up a fight.

Stephen punched the killer's face, which caused the mask to crack. He wasn't the strongest person, though, so the hit didn't daze the killer. He kicked the killer's stomach, pushing the intruder to the farthest wall in the restroom. He punched him again, then he leaned closer and tried to grab the mask. He figured if he died during the confrontation, he would at least feel more comfortable if he knew the killer's identity.

The killer grabbed Stephen's jaw with his right hand and pushed him away while pulling his own head back until he hit the wall. He was clearly defensive about his identity. With his left hand, he retrieved a switchblade from his pocket. With the press of a button, a three-and-a-half-inch blade protruded from the handle. He stabbed the stoner twice in the lower abdomen. He even twisted the blade during the second stabbing.

Stephen took a deep breath. He furrowed his brow as he stared down at the killer's hand. He felt as if he were just punched. Then, he saw the blood soaking through his shirt. A twinge reverberated from his stomach, causing his entire body to shudder. He felt pain—*pure pain.* He gritted his teeth and held his hands over his wounds. A vein bulged from his brow as he held his breath.

He staggered away from the killer, who appeared calm throughout the stabbing. The stoner glanced down at Dominique as he stepped over her body. To his dismay, he knew he couldn't save her. He stumbled into the corridor, debilitated by the pain, then he lurched down the hallway and headed back to Wilson's class.

As he ran, Stephen murmured, "I'm sorry, Dom..."

The masked person grabbed Dominique's ankles and dragged her deeper into the restroom. Dominique wept hysterically as the shears were pulled out of her back. The killer tossed them aside, then he stepped towards the victim's head. He knelt down in front of her.

Although she tried to pull away, the killer grabbed a fistful of her hair and turned her head towards him. He held his index and middle fingers up to his eyes, as if to say: *look into my eyes.*

Dominique gazed into her attacker's eyes, baffled. Her bottom lip quivered as tears streamed down her rosy cheeks. The fear clinging to her pupils was blatant.

In a croaky tone, she stuttered, "I–I know you. Oh, no, I... *I know you.*" The killer nodded, then he stood to his feet. As her attacker lifted his boot over her head, Dominique stammered, "Pl–Pl–Please, don't–don't do this. I'm so–"

Mid-sentence, the killer stomped on the nape of Dominique's neck—breaking her spine and crushing her throat with the brutal stomping. He lifted his foot up, then he stomped her again. Two gashes formed on each side of her neck. Blood leaked from the gashes and spilled on the floor like soup from an overflowing bowl. A large, boot-sized indentation formed on her neck—a crater. That crater caused her chin to lift up from the floor and cocked her head up, her hollow eyes staring at nothing.

Chapter Seventeen

Love & Tragedy

"He killed her!" Stephen shouted as he lurched down the hallway. Eyes welling over with tears, he yelled, "We have to leave! We... We have to get the hell out of here! Fuck!"

Hand on his stomach, Stephen staggered into the doorway of the classroom. Coughing and grunting, he leaned on the doorway as he stared into the room. His vision was blurred by his tears, but he could see four figures in the classroom—his friends and the teacher. They all appeared to be standing and holding textbooks, ready to fight any intruder.

Wilson shined his light at the doorway. He dropped his textbook on the table and said, "It's just you. What are you screaming about, kid? What–" He stopped upon spotting the blood on Stephen's hands and shirt. He asked, "Is... Is that blood?"

Stephen nodded and said, "He... He stabbed me. That bastard shanked me in the restroom, man! We have to get out of here!"

Teary-eyed, Charlene stepped forward and asked, "What happened over there, Stephen? Who did this to you? Where's Dominique?"

"Who did this to me? A bastard in a mask... Fuck, man, he got Dominique, too. We need to leave. *Now*."

Wilson rushed to Stephen's side. He gently slapped the boy's cheek and asked, "What did you just say? Huh? What happened to Dominique?

Where is she?" Stephen breathed throatily as he struggled to cope with the pain. Wilson hit him again and asked, "Where is Dominique? What do you mean he 'got' her? Talk to us, damn it."

Stephen pulled away from the teacher. He said, "Shit... Stop hitting me. I told you: *he got her.* I didn't see her die, but I saw her dying. She was... She was on the restroom floor. There was blood everywhere. She couldn't move, man. I didn't know what to do. I tried to fight him, but... I couldn't do it. I–I was too weak."

His bottom lip trembling, Wilson stepped in reverse. He was shocked by the devastating news. His high school lover was either dead or dying. Either way, their future was no longer bright. Everything would be revealed in due time.

Seizing the opportunity, Adam stepped forward and said, "It was you. You killed her, didn't you?"

Stephen grimaced and said, "No. *No,* man. I'm fucking bleeding over here. I'm dying!"

"That doesn't mean shit. That could be fake blood. Hell, you could have asked your partner to stab you, just like the movie."

"P–Partner?"

"Don't lie to us. You sold weed to Nico once, didn't you? You're helping him now, aren't you?"

"No. That's wrong."

"It's right."

Charlene pulled on Adam's arm and asked, "What are you doing? You're not thinking straight."

Adam responded, "I *am* thinking straight, Charles. He knows where we all live, he knows all of our numbers. He just left with Dominique and now she's dying. Can't you see? It all leads to him." He grabbed Charlene's hand and dragged her away. He said, "We have to get out of here."

Charlene tried to pull away from his grip, but to no avail—Adam was just too strong. As she was pulled out of the room, she took one final glance at Stephen. From the look in his eyes—a look of sincere fear—she knew he wasn't capable of killing them. Yet, against her will, she followed Adam's lead.

Britney glanced at Wilson, then at Stephen. She refused to stay with the men. She whimpered as she ran out of the room and followed the couple.

Stephen glanced over at Wilson and weakly said, "You... You have to call 911. Help... Help me. Please, don't leave me."

Wilson jabbed his index finger at Stephen's face and said, "If you laid a single finger on her... I swear, I'll make you pay."

The teacher slipped out of the room, then he ran down the hall. While his students took a left and ran towards the front of the school, he ran towards another corridor to his right and headed to the girls' restroom to save Dominique.

With a trembling hand, Stephen flicked the light switch and illuminated the classroom. He hoped the light would attract the police. He couldn't do much more, though. He was running out of energy. He fell to his knees and indistinctly mumbled to himself as he waited for the rescue party—*or death.*

***

Wilson slowed from a jog to a stroll as he approached the restroom. Light poured through the open doorway and illuminated the corridor. He couldn't hear a struggle in the restroom, though. Aside from the buzzing lights, he didn't hear anything at all. The silence was horrifying.

He stopped at the doorway, shocked. Tears dripped from his eyes with each rapid blink. He wheezed and mumbled indistinctly, his mouth flooded with saliva. His legs wobbled, his heart raced, and his teeth chattered. He was heartbroken by his horrific discovery.

Dominique lay on the floor, brutalized. Due to her broken neck, her head was cocked up and tilted to the side. Her chin rested on the linoleum floor. Puddles of blood formed under her neck and waist. A *plopping* sound emerged in the room as blood dripped from her wounds. A moist *squelching* sound emerged from her body, too.

As he took his first step into the restroom, Wilson stuttered, "Wh–Who... Who did..." He tightly closed his eyes and grunted, overwhelmed by his sadness. He barked, "Who did this to you?! God, who could do such a thing? Why... Why would someone do this? *Why?!*"

Barbaric murder often did not have answers. He fell to his knees in front of Dominique's body. He held his trembling hands over her head, afraid to touch her—as if she were a gentle artifact that would crumble with the slightest touch. Still, he couldn't resist. His heart told him to attempt to soothe her pain, despite her death. He gently caressed her cheek, as if he were trying to comfort her.

He leaned closer to her ear and whispered, "I'm sorry, princess. I loved you. I always loved you. We should have never came here. We should have ran off, baby. Why didn't we just run away? Why didn't we leave this damn city behind? They would have never understood our love anyway. I'm sorry..."

The sound of thudding footsteps approached. The steps stopped behind the tragic scene of love and death.

Wilson, trembling with rage, said, "Stephen... Stephen, you bastard dope-head. I'm going to kill you." He staggered to his feet and shouted, "I'm going to kill you! I'm–"

He stopped as he glanced over his shoulder. He found himself staring at an uninvited guest. The burly person wore a black raincoat, dark jeans and a white Bauta paper-mâché mask—the same mask the person wore when he killed Michael. His sharp blue eyes matched the angry expression on the painted mask.

Wilson was awed. He had never seen the killer before. He read the news, he heard the rumors, but he didn't watch any of the videos. Seeing the mask in the restroom flooded his mind with a thousand complex thoughts. His students weren't lying—he recognized the mask. It belonged to Casey. *It can't be Stephen,* the teacher thought, *he couldn't have changed so fast, right?*

A lump of anxiety forming in his throat, Wilson asked, "Who are you? Why are you doing this?" The killer did not respond. As he wiped the tears from his eyes, Wilson asked, "Nico, is that you? Have you been doing this for... for your brother? For Casey?"

Again, the killer did not respond.

Wilson took another step forward. He slowly

lifted his hands in a peaceful gesture, hoping to calm the killer. He wanted to stop the masked person from attacking while extracting information from him. He sought an upper-hand—an advantage.

The sound of blood plopping on the floor echoed through the room. The sound was minuscule, but it was loud to the teacher. Each *plop* was louder than the last. The dripping sound drilled into his ears, like the shrill sound of nails scratching a chalkboard.

Wilson closed his eyes and gritted his teeth, trying his best to contain his anger. He couldn't ignore the tragic facts, though. His girlfriend was viciously slaughtered and the masked person was responsible—he was certain of that.

Wilson wagged his finger at the intruder and, through his gritted teeth, he said, "You bastard... You can't kill people like this because... because of what happened. You're sick. You... You..." He grunted and groaned, infuriated. He barked, "You're a sick bastard! I'll kill you!"

As Wilson ran towards the doorway, the killer raised his right hand from behind his back, revealing the taser in his hand. Without any hesitation, he pulled the trigger. Wilson didn't have the opportunity to dodge the attack. The prongs penetrated the teacher's stomach and shocked him, causing him to tumble to the floor.

Wilson's body tightened, his limbs locked in place. He shuddered uncontrollably and indistinctly mumbled, stunned by the attack.

The killer stepped over his body. He pulled Wilson's arms back. A *clicking* sound echoed through the room as he tightly handcuffed his wrists behind his back. He didn't waste any time, either. He handcuffed his ankles, then he dragged him closer to Dominique's body. He forced the lovers to lay in the same puddle of blood—one was alive, the other dead.

As he cried, Wilson asked, "What... What do you want from me? Why are you doing this?"

The masked person knelt down in front of Wilson. His glistening eyes, moist with tears, could be seen through the holes on his mask. He reached into his coat pocket, then he pulled out a neatly folded piece of paper.

With narrowed eyes, Wilson watched as the intruder unfolded the paper. His eyes widened upon reading the sheet. The killer held a printed news article from the previous year. The title read: *Local teacher tried to stop bullying of suicide victim, hailed as a hero.* The article referred to Casey Marshall's tragic suicide. Collin Wilson, Casey's teacher, was the supposed hero. The mere fact that he *tried* to help was enough to win over the public.

The killer clenched his fist and crumpled the paper. He tossed it aside, then he pulled another folded sheet from his coat pocket.

Wilson's eyes watered as he stared at the second article, horrified. The headline read: *Hero teacher reaches publishing deal, hopes to help students cope with bullying.* The second article revealed the sad truth about the situation. Wilson was susceptible to human flaw. He saw an opportunity and he took it. He didn't save Casey, but he happily capitalized off of his death. He used his student's suicide to propel himself to a B-list celebrity status.

Tragedy—the death of the innocent—sold books.

Tears streaming across his cheeks, Wilson said, "I didn't hurt him. I really tried to help him, but... but these assholes wouldn't leave him alone. I tried. Everything else, it... it was a mistake. I needed money. I–I... I really wanted to help other kids, too. You have to believe me." He glanced over at Dominique and wheezed. He stared back at the killer and stuttered, "He–He wouldn't want this. He was... He was a good kid. Please, don't hurt me."

The killer crushed the paper, then he tossed it aside—never taking his eyes off of the greedy teacher.

In a hoarse tone, raspy and sonorous, the masked person said, "You didn't help him. You're no hero. You're a piece of shit... and shit must be flushed."

"Wha–What? Wait... Wait a second, damn it! Don't do this! Don't–"

The killer pulled a large Bowie knife from a holster under his coat. Without saying a word, he stabbed Wilson's stomach below his belly button.

Veins bulging from his neck and brow, Wilson gasped. He panted like a dog during a hot summer, his lungs vacuumed with the stabbing.

The killer wiggled the knife up-and-down as he slid the blade across the teacher's stomach. With each wiggle of the blade, he widened the deep wound. Blood squirted onto his coat and spilled onto the floor, but it did not deter him. He was determined. He sawed Wilson's stomach from one hip to the other. He hooked his arms under the teacher's armpits, then he dragged him into the neighboring stall.

Wilson's head swayed every which way, dazed due to the loss of blood. His vision was blurred and his breathing was erratic.

The killer shoved his fingers into Wilson's wound. He used his fingers to widen the gash on his stomach until he could see his organs. He twisted the blade, cutting through the teacher's thick abdominal muscles. He reached for Wilson's small intestine. He didn't have time to find the beginning or end of the long organ, so he cut through it—he made his own end.

With flickering eyelids, Wilson watched as blood spilled from the gaping hole on his stomach. He panted as the killer began pulling his small intestine out of the hole. He was in shock—utter disbelief. He felt as if the situation was impossible, but it was happening—and no one could say anything about it. He watched his own disembowelment.

The killer tossed the end of the small intestine into the toilet while the organ was still connected to Wilson's body. He gazed into Wilson's eyes, savoring the fear in his soul, then he flushed the toilet.

Wilson's legs trembled as his small intestine quickly unwrapped itself and swam down the pipe. *Thud*—the deep, sonorous sound echoed through the room as the organ clogged the toilet.

Wilson's bloodied guts were slung over his shoulder and *clogged* in the toilet—still attached to his body. The bloody water started to rise in the bowl, then it spilled over the edge. Groaning and squelching sounds emerged from the toilet. The teacher vacantly stared at the ceiling, blood dripping from the corner of his mouth.

The killer gazed into Wilson's hollow eyes. He wanted to memorize every detail of his gruesome death. He shook his head, then he walked away. His boots splashed on the water and blood on the floor. His squeaky steps echoed through the empty school as he exited the restroom.

The massacre was not over. There were still three targets on campus.

Chapter Eighteen

No Escape

Charlene, Adam, and Britney sprinted down the hallway, ignoring the sound of Stephen's crying and Wilson's footsteps. Charlene and Britney stopped near the front entrance while Adam clashed with the doors. The doors rattled, but they didn't open.

Adam glanced at the bottom of the doors, then at the top. He pushed the door again and murmured, "What the hell? Are we locked in?"

Surprised, Charlene repeated, "*Locked in?*" She rushed forward and peered through the windows on the door to the left—a chain and a padlock were wrapped around the handles outside. She said, "Oh, shit, you're right. Someone locked us in from the outside. It... It doesn't make any sense. If someone locked us in from out there and attacked us in here, then there must be someone el–"

"Enough of the investigative bullshit, Charlene," Adam snapped, clearly frustrated. He kicked the door, then he tossed his body at the barrier—but to no avail. He shouted, "Fuck! Piece of shit!"

"Calm down, Adam. Do you want to draw him—*or them*—to us? Huh? We have to think about this."

"You're right, you're right. We have to think about how we're going to get the hell out of here. No more of your goddamn theories. They've gotten us into enough trouble. Drop it. Just drop it. Okay... We're... Damn it, what the hell are we going to do?"

Charlene grabbed Adam's hand and said, "The first thing we have to do is go back to Wilson's classroom and get Stephen. We *have* to help him."

Adam shook his head and said, "No. No, fuck that. He could be the killer. I'm not risking my life to help some drug-dealing psychopath. I can't do that."

"He's not the killer, Adam. We both know that. He couldn't hurt a fly. He's soft. He's always been soft. And, even if he was somehow capable of killing all of those people, it would be better if we kept him in our sights—but he's *not* the killer. He's our friend. We can't leave him back there. We can't let him die like that. Let's help him. Please."

Adam gazed into Charlene's eyes, baffled by her ability to trust during the most hectic times. He could see something else in her eyes, too—*passion.* She truly cared about Stephen. *Does she love the stoner?*–he thought.

Adam slowly shook his head and said, "I can't do that. Not for him, not for you, not for anyone."

Teary-eyed, Charlene took a step in reverse and tilted her head to the side. Just as Adam was amazed by her unwavering kindness, she was shocked by his heartless response.

Sensing an argument brewing, Britney stepped forward and said, "I care about Stephen and Dominique... and even Wilson, but we can't stand around here and do nothing. We have to find a way out of here. The sooner we're out, the sooner we can get help. It's not like we can stop the bleeding. We need the police, the paramedics... *everyone.*"

Wide-eyed, Charlene glanced at Britney and asked, "Did you call the cops?" Britney shook her head. Charlene said, "We have to call 911. No one ever does it in the movies because they're all contrived and shit. We have cell phones, though. We have brains. Call 911. *Hurry.*"

Before Britney could pull her phone out of her pocket, Adam grabbed her arm and pulled her closer to him. The look in his eyes was feral—evil in its purest form.

He sternly said, "We don't have time to call the cops right now. What are they going to do? Teleport here? We have to leave before that psycho catches us. Okay?" Tears dripping from her eyes with each blink, Britney rapidly nodded—*okay.* The young man released her and said, "The front door is locked. We can't go through the back 'cause Dominique died near there."

Britney stuttered, "The–The windows in the classrooms won't open wide enough for us to fit, either. We... We can't just jump out of a window."

"So, that only leaves the emergency exits."

"Wait. What if he locked all of those doors, too?"

"Then we're fucked. We have to try, though. If we stay here, we die. We can either go to the exit to the east or west. I think we should try the gym's emergency exit. No one ever uses that one and he probably forgot it."

Britney nodded and said, "That sounds like a plan."

Before they could leave, Charlene said, "Wait." She stepped in front of Adam and said, "I can't believe you. You... You're actually willing to leave and abandon everyone just to save your own ass? Stephen is our friend, Adam, and he needs us. We have to go back for him. Don't make me beg. I'll–"

"Guys," Britney interrupted in a soft, cracking voice.

The arguing couple turned towards her. Adam raised his brow and Charlene tilted her head as they stared at her. Britney pointed down the hall, her arm trembling uncontrollably.

Britney stuttered, "He–He's here..."

The group stared down the hall, terrified. Through the darkness, they could see a figure in the distance. The silhouette stood out against the darkness—mysterious and malevolent. He did not appear as large as the stories described. He didn't move, either.

Holding Charlene's hand, Adam stepped forward and whispered, "It's him. It's really him..."

A dim light illuminated the mysterious person's hand and stomach as well as the surrounding lockers. He appeared to be using a small device, tapping and swiping—as if he were scrolling through a page on a phone or composing a text message. Yet, he did not move forward and attack.

His behavior—natural under any other circumstance—was eerie. For a moment, just a second, the figure did not appear human. His slight, creepy movements, which allowed him to blend seamlessly with the shadows, appeared monstrous. He was the bogeyman—the monster everyone feared.

The group shared the same thought: *why isn't he attacking us?*

As the intruder aimed the device at the group, Britney asked, "What is he doing?"

Charlene said, "I... I think he's recording us."

Before they could utter another word, the figure started running towards them.

In a slapdash reaction, Britney ran through the doorway to her right. Without thinking of her friends, she locked the door behind her. The young woman ended up in the administration area—*cornered.*

Still holding Charlene's hand, Adam ran forward and led his girlfriend to the intersection of hallways in front of them. Before the killer could reach them, the couple ran down the corridor to the right. They headed west, hurtling towards the gym.

Chapter Nineteen

Administration

Britney leaned back on the door, breathing heavily through her nose as she tried to compose herself. She glanced around the room and searched for an exit. She had been there before, but it all seemed alien to her—as if she had miraculously stepped into a different dimension when she ran through the doorway.

A row of seats hugged the wall to the right—the seating area. To her left, there was a long reception counter. Behind the counter, there were a few desks, which were used by some faculty members and a few student aides. Beyond the desks, there were several offices for the counselors and principal.

She wouldn't be able to escape through the windows in the offices, but she would be able to hide. She thought about fighting, but she knew she would lose. Hiding was her only option.

Britney ran around the reception counter. She sprinted towards the principal's office, but she skidded to a stop before she could reach the door. A thought dawned onto her: *the police,* no one ever called in the movies because it was too contrived. She glanced over at the tables. The landline phone called to her with honeyed words—*use me.*

She hunched down beside the desk. She held the landline phone to her ear, pushing the coiled cord aside as she dialed 911. She hopped in place and stared at the door, anxious. The call connected.

A female operator asked, "911, what is your emergency?"

Britney stuttered, "He–He's killing... He's killing all of my friends. They're all dying. Please, send help."

"Where are you, ma'am? Are you in any immediate danger?"

"Yes! The killer is here... The masked man who killed Tiffany, Anna, Michael... *He's here.* He's going to–"

"Where are you, ma'am?" the operator interrupted.

"Redwood High School. Our teacher snuck us in. I'm calling from–from the administration area. Okay? My friends... They're somewhere else in the school. Some of them are dead, too. You have to hurry. He's coming for me. I know it."

In a calm tone, professional but sympathetic, the operator said, "Okay, ma'am. The police are on their way. Right now, I need you to exit the building if you can. If not, you need to hide. When the officers arrive, you have to comply. Don't–"

Britney gasped as the door began to rattle. She sobbed and wheezed, losing control of herself as death banged on the door.

She cried, "He's already here... I'm going to die, but... I don't want to die. Not like this..."

The operator responded, "Ma'am, if you're in danger, you need to hide—*now.* Drop the phone, squeeze yourself into someplace he can't reach, and stay quiet. The police are on their way."

Britney slammed the phone on the table and

glanced around the room. She searched for a hiding place, but the rattling of the door distorted her thoughts. A deep *thud* echoed through the area as the intruder kicked at the door with all of his might. The sound grew louder with each kick. It sounded as if the door would explode off its hinges at any second.

The clock was ticking and death was approaching.

The young woman ran into the principal's office —the last room to the right. She slinked into the room, then she carefully closed the door. She tried to stay as quiet as possible. Just as she closed the door, the door to the administration area swung open after a powerful punt. She barely evaded the intruder's eyesight.

Britney held her hands over her mouth as she tried to control her breathing. She stared into the administration area through the thin window pane next to the door. She gasped and hid behind the door as the lights turned on—the killer wasn't dim, he wasn't going to search in the dark. She peeked through the window again.

Just as the rumors described, a person in a raincoat and masked searched under the desks in the administration area. The mask caught her eye: a paper-mâché plague doctor mask.

Britney whimpered as she stared down at the handle of the door. To her dismay, she forgot to turn the lock on the door. She thought about turning the lock at that moment, but the unavoidable *clicking* sound would only attract the killer. She needed every second she could buy. She fell to her knees, then she crawled across the small office. She pushed the principal's rolling chair aside, then she squeezed herself under the desk.

They'll be here any second now, she thought, *it won't take longer than five minutes, I know it.*

As she listened to the sounds of the killer flipping desks and breaking computers, Britney pulled her cell phone out. In tears, she opened her text messages. Her fingers trembled as she composed a message to her mother.

The message read: *I love you, mom. I love you so much. I'm so scared. I don't think I'm going to make it.* She paused and sniffled, then she wrote another message to her mother. The second message read: *I'm sorry for taking your car. I'm sorry for everything. I love you. I love all of you.*

Britney wheezed as she struggled to come to terms with her inevitable death. By typing the messages, she felt as if she had given up on life— and, in a sense, *she did.* She opened another message thread. Tears dripped from her eyes as she read over the messages she shared with Charlene. The memories were bittersweet. She sent a text message to her best friend.

The message read: *He's in the administration area, Charles. Get out. Get out alive. I love you, sweetie.*

She gasped and pulled the phone closer to her chest as the door swung open. She placed one hand over her mouth and held her breath. She shoved the phone into her pocket, trying to hide the light from the screen. She leaned closer to the floor and gazed at the doorway from under the desk. Her eyes widened with fear as she spotted the killer's steel-toe boots.

He stood in the doorway, motionless. His refusal to move was eerie. He was purposely trying to frighten Britney—he was fucking with her. *How long can you hold your breath, darling?*

Britney panted through her nose, struggling to keep her composure. She shuddered uncontrollably. The windows were closed, but she still felt an icy sensation across her body—her blood chilled. With a *clicking* sound, a wave of light illuminated the room. The killer finally stepped forward. She could see his slow and calculated steps as he approached the desk. He stopped in front of the table. A few *thuds* emerged from the tabletop.

Britney couldn't see it, but it sounded like the intruder was playing with the principal's knick-knacks. He moved the phone, his pen basket, his picture frame, and everything else on his desk. He wasn't searching for anything, though. He was just reminiscing about the past—he had been there before. The memories weren't great, though.

Britney trembled uncontrollably as the intruder knocked on the desk. She breathed deeply through her nose, trying her best to contain herself.

The intruder knocked again. He grabbed one side of the desk, then he flipped the table—effortlessly hurling the desk at the neighboring wall and exposing Britney's position.

Britney crawled towards a bookcase behind the principal's chair. With bloodshot eyes, she cried, "No, please don't hurt me. Don't kill me, mister. I... I didn't do anything wrong. Don't hurt me!"

The intruder glared at her. She could see his

furious eyes through the holes on his mask. Forgiveness was not an option. He grabbed the thick cord from the landline phone. As he approached, Britney staggered to her feet and stumbled towards the door. Before she could even reach the center of the room, the masked person tossed the cable over her head, then he pulled it back at her throat.

Britney coughed and grunted as she was strangled. She fell to her knees while the intruder stood behind her, tugging on the cable with all of his might. Britney scratched at her throat, trying to dig her nails under the thick cord to no avail. Her nails sliced into her neck, causing blood to stream over the cord and down to her chest.

The blood only made it more difficult for her to grip the cord. Yet, she couldn't stop herself. Her nails continued to penetrate her skin as she tried to stop the strangulation. She was fighting for survival after all. The couple locked eyes—Britney's eyes bulged from her skull while the killer's eyes remained livid.

In a hoarse tone, the killer said, "You had a big mouth. You should have stayed off the damn phone. You should have left him alone."

Struggling to breathe, Britney furrowed her brow and tilted her head as she stared up at her attacker. Despite the struggle, she understood his statement. She just couldn't believe it. Hoarse gasps escaped her lips as she painfully suffocated. Aside from an involuntary twitch, she stopped wrestling with the intruder.

The masked person, still pulling on the cord with one hand, knelt down and grabbed the principal's nib pen from the floor. The sharp tip was perfect.

The intruder said, "The things you said about the things you never saw... All of it for 'likes' and attention. You're sick. You're disgusting. You shouldn't be allowed to talk anymore and you shouldn't be allowed to see. Your eyes *can't* be trusted."

He lifted the pen over his shoulder with the nib pointing downward, the back of Britney's head resting on his knee. Eyes wide with fear, she shuddered as she stared at the sharp point of the pen. Suffocating, she didn't have the opportunity to scream. She was too weak to fight or run. She could only watch in horror.

The killer stabbed Britney's left eye with the pen. Her eye immediately reddened. She panted and flailed her limbs every which way as the killer removed the pen. He wasn't finished, though. He stabbed *under* her left eye, slicing through her eyelid and penetrating her eye socket. He wiggled the pen in her socket, trying his best to scoop her eye out.

Blood squirted from her eye and streamed down her cheek—bloody tears, just like his mask. As he sawed into her eye, Britney fell limp. The lack of oxygen and the sheer shock killed her.

Yet, the masked killer continued to cut into her eye. He grunted and groaned in frustration. Anger clearly fueled his rampage—and it wasn't over.

Chapter Twenty

The Truth

Charlene and Adam ran through the double-door entrance of the gym. Adam, visibly worried, refused to release Charlene's hand during their entire run. Charlene, however, was not willing to leave without her friends. She stopped running and leaned back, forcing Adam to stumble near the center of the court.

As soon as he regained his footing, Adam glanced back at Charlene with wide eyes. Charlene stood her ground and shook her head.

Adam asked, "What are you doing? The exit is right there. We have to go. *Now.*"

"I'm not going anywhere without our friends. I have to make sure Britney is okay, I have to go back and help Stephen."

"Britney can take care of herself and we can't trust Stephen. We've been through this already. Let's go."

"*No.*"

Adam stared at his girlfriend in disbelief. Some would call it 'compassion,' he would call it 'stupidity.' Although he cared about the girl, he wasn't going to be another horror movie victim. He bit his bottom lip, then he sprinted towards the emergency exit at the other end of the gym.

As she watched him run, Charlene shouted, "You selfish asshole!"

Adam slipped and slid as he approached the exit. He couldn't help but smile. *The finish line,* he thought, *I reached the end.* He lunged forward and tackled the exit—but to no avail. The door rattled in the frame, but it didn't budge. He stepped in reverse, awed. He stood on his tiptoes and peered through the window on the door.

The door was chained.

As he staggered in reverse, Adam whispered, "It's... It's locked. Why did he lock this door?"

Charlene said, "I knew it would end this way. He wasn't going to let us walk out of this place without a fight. He's a step ahead. He's *always* been a step ahead of us." She glanced around the empty gym, saddened. She said, "Someone is helping him. I know it. How else would he know we were here? It's... It's just not possible."

Adam grabbed Charlene's hand and said, "Come on, we can't be standing out here in the open. We have to hide until help arrives."

He tugged on his girlfriend's arm. The young woman reluctantly followed his lead. The couple ended up under the retracting bleachers—the same bleachers they sat on during the assembly. It was dark, eerie, and cramped under the seats.

In a soft tone, Charlene asked, "Do you really think Stephen is capable of killing all of those people? *Stephen?* The guy who smokes weed and watches horror movies all day? Hmm?"

"Does it matter?"

"What? Of course it matters. We left him behind. He could be dead."

"We did what we had to do to survive. Okay? No

matter what way you put it, Stephen is guilty. If he didn't kill anyone, he probably did something just as bad. People have to pay for their sins, Charlene. I don't think it's fair, but that's just the way the world works."

Wide-eyed, Charlene responded, "*What?* What the hell are you talking about, Adam? Do you know something I–"

She stopped as the doors swung open in the gym. The sound of *thudding* footsteps echoed through the area, slow and calculated. The footsteps grew louder, then they dwindled in sound as the person approached the other end of the gym. The sound of the emergency exit rattling emerged. It wasn't a sound of panic, though.

The fact bothered Charlene. She wanted to believe Stephen or Britney had made it to the exit. She knew that idea was nothing but a fallacy. The intruder had arrived—and he brought death with him.

Charlene leaned closer to Adam and whispered, "What do we do? Can we fight him? Should we–"

Adam held his finger up to Charlene's lips— *shush.* He glanced around. There were two possible exits under the bleachers. The killer would have to emerge from one end, so they'd just run out from the other side. The escape plan was simple and effective. However, if all of the emergency exits were locked, they would only be able to run around in circles in the school.

No matter what, they were still trapped in the building.

The couple glanced over to their left as the sound

of footsteps emerged again. The killer was approaching the bleachers. One, two, three... *ten steps*—the intruder stopped near the seating area. He didn't move again. Silence reigned supreme as the couple stared at the end of the bleachers, waiting for death to arrive.

Like a curious turtle, the intruder poked his head around the corner and gazed into the area under the bleachers.

Charlene gasped and stepped in reverse upon spotting his Bauta paper-mâché mask. The angry expression startled her. She could see his glimmering blue eyes through the darkness, too. Her eyes widened upon spotting the bloody Bowie knife in his right hand.

The couple stared at the masked person, incapable of moving. The intruder stared back at them, stationary but furious. He took his first step froward, crouching under the bleachers. Yet, the couple remained motionless—deer in the headlights, targets in the crosshairs.

***

As Adam took his first step back, prepared to run at the first opportunity, Charlene stepped forward and said, "I'm not running from you... not until I know the truth. Did you kill Dominique? Did you attack Stephen? Wilson? *Britney?*"

The intruder tilted his head to the left as he stared at Charlene. He nodded—*yes, I attacked them.* He stepped closer to the couple, but the young woman stood her ground.

Charlene asked, "*Why?* What did we do to deserve this? Huh? What did Anna, Tiffany, Michael... What did any of us do to deserve this?" The killer stopped in his tracks, silent but curious. Charlene nodded and said, "Yeah. You don't have an answer, do you? You're just another psychopath killing innocent people. You... You're a sick bastard! You hear me? You don't deserve to live! I hate you!"

Still, the killer did not move. Adam pushed his girlfriend from behind, causing her to stagger down to her knees in front of the killer. Charlene glanced back at Adam, shocked by his betrayal.

Zany-eyed, Adam said, "Kill her. I did everything you asked me to do. I told you where they were, what they were doing... Fuck, man, I even helped bring them here. I held up my end of the bargain. If you want her, *take her.* I'm done with this. It's over."

Awed, Charlene stared at Adam with sorrowful eyes and stuttered, "You–You've been... You've been helping him this whole time? It was... It was you? You bastard..."

"It was us," the masked person said. "It was all of us."

Charlene glanced back at the intruder, surprised.

The killer lifted his mask over the hood of his jacket, revealing his face. A young man stood before the couple—seventeen, maybe eighteen years old. He had a chiseled, clean-shaved face. He was clearly a lean, strong person. Locks of his wavy black hair protruded from under the hood, falling over his moist forehead. His blue eyes revealed the pain and anger in his soul.

"I'm tired of masks. I love these with all of my heart, but they're tacky. They're not good for this, either," the killer said. "You deserve to know why you're being punished. Being punished without reason is pointless... I've been hiding the *truth* in me for so long. It has to come out. Everyone has to know about this. Besides, it's not like I can kill you both at the same time. I'm sure one of you will get away for a minute while I talk... but I'll still come after you. I'll come after you until you're all dead."

As she stared at him, Charlene said, "Nico... You're Nico Marshall, aren't you?"

The killer did not respond. He appeared to be lost in his thoughts—thoughts of the past.

"That's exactly who he is. Wasn't it obvious from the beginning?" Adam said in a condescending tone, blatantly anxious. He nodded at his partner and said, "I did what you asked me to do. I got all of the bullies for you. I handed them to you on a silver *fuckin'* platter. I did it, Nico. You said you wouldn't bother me. You said this would make us even. Why is that emergency door locked? That wasn't part of the deal."

Nico remained quiet as he stared at Adam, reading every twitch on his face and every shudder on his body. Adam stared back at Nico, hoping to conjure a sense of sympathy in the wicked killer. The pair had a deal—but it wasn't carved in stone.

Charlene stared up at Nico and said, "This was about Casey... You did all of this for your brother, didn't you?"

Nico said, "We all have history together. Everyone who died this past month... They *deserved* to die. All of them contributed to the toxic gossip of this shitty high school 'culture.' If you can even call it a culture..." He nervously chuckled, clearly deranged.

He glared at Adam and said, "It's amazing, isn't it? All of this started with a rumor—a rumor *you* started. And now you think you deserve to walk away without being punished? You're an idiot. A fucking idiot..."

Charlene furrowed her brow upon hearing the revelation. She was aware of Casey's suicide, but she didn't know all of the details. Bullying killed him— that was what she always believed. She glanced back at Adam—confused, frightened, *disgusted.*

As he glanced around the underbelly of the bleachers, Nico said, "It all started here, too. My brother hid down here after he was jumped by Michael and Kyle. I came down here and tried to talk to him, I tried to make him feel better... But, that's not what you told everyone, was it, Adam?" Adam stared down at himself, ashamed. Eyes welling over with tears, Nico continued, "For some reason, you told people you saw me *fucking* my brother—and they believed you. These idiots actually believed you... From there, it just spread like wildfire, just like everything does on social media. You told Anna, Anna told Tiffany, Tiffany told Hailey, Hailey told Stephen, Stephen told Dominique, and Dominique told Britney... Everyone told someone!"

Charlene stumbled back, surprised by Nico's bellow of pain. She staggered to her feet. She gasped as she bumped into Adam. She teetered away from him, too. The truth tainted her vision of him—he was a bad person.

She felt a strong vibration in her pocket. As she cautiously moved towards the exit, she pulled her phone out. She just received a message from Britney.

The message read: *He's in the administration area, Charles. Get out. Get out alive. I love you, sweetie.*

Charlene shuddered as she read the message. *How can he be in two places at once?*–she thought. She blinked erratically as she struggled to comprehend the situation.

Nico turned his attention to Charlene and said, "People like you just stood around and watched. You didn't help spread the rumors, but you listened to them and you did nothing to stop them. You're just as guilty. After all of those years, being beaten and ignored, Casey finally took his own life. It wasn't fair. All of you have to die..."

Nico took a step forward, knife in hand. Adam didn't move, though. Charlene staggered in reverse, teetering towards the other end of the bleachers. *This is it,* she thought, *he's going to kill one of us.*

Interrupting her thoughts, Adam said, "It's over, Nico." Charlene glanced over at her boyfriend and saw the partners standing face-to-face. Adam continued, "The truth is out. Spreading a lie isn't a crime, but killing people is. I think you've killed enough, man. You don't have to do this. I told you before: it was just supposed to be a joke. I'm sorry. What else do–"

Mid-sentence, Nico thrust the large knife through Adam's chin and *into* his mouth. The blade ripped through the muscle and tissue. The knife sliced half of his tongue, too. Blood spilled from his mouth and streamed across his neck.

Adam, shocked by the attack, staggered to his knees. He fell limp and leaned on Nico's legs. He mumbled indistinctly as he glanced around. He couldn't form a single comprehensible sentence, though—a garble of noise spewed from his mouth along with plenty of blood.

Nico crouched beside his victim. He grabbed the handle of the blade, then he began sawing into Adam's jaw. He planned on ripping his jaw and tongue off.

As he vigorously sawed through the tendons and ligaments, Nico gritted his teeth and said, "You don't... deserve... to speak."

Charlene held her hands over her mouth as she watched the violent attack. She wanted to scream, she thought about running, but she was paralyzed by her fear. Only one thought ran through her mind: *I'm next.*

The motorized bleachers rumbled, then the seats retracted—one row at a time. Charlene glanced over her shoulder. She couldn't help but smile as she spotted Stephen at the end of the bleachers. The stoner didn't abandon his friends.

Still holding his stomach, Stephen beckoned to Charlene and shouted, "Let's go!"

Charlene crouched under the seats, then she stumbled out from under the bleachers. She placed her palms on Stephen's cheeks and planted a kiss on his lips—*thank you.* She wrapped her arm around his waist and helped him hobble across the basketball court.

As the bleachers retracted towards him, Nico yelled, "Charlene! Stephen! Don't run from me, you bastards! You owe me! You owe my brother!"

He firmly grabbed Adam's bottom teeth, then he violently tugged on his jaw. A wave of blood spilled on the floor as he ripped his jaw from his face. His partially-severed tongue dangled over his remaining jaw. The killer threw the detached jaw aside, then he ran forward. As he slipped out from under the bleachers, he spotted Charlene and Stephen running back into the school corridors.

Nico shouted, "Get back here!"

Charlene and Stephen hobbled down the hall and headed back to the main entrance. They didn't have any other options. Stephen leaned on the lockers and dragged his feet. Despite Charlene's help, he could barely walk due to his severe loss of blood. Down the hall, past five classrooms and an intersection, they could see the finish line—the main entrance. The doors appeared to be open, too, as moonlight poured into the hallway.

Stephen pushed Charlene away from him and said, "Run. Hurry, Charles."

Charlene gazed into Stephen's eyes, reluctant. She could see he was sincere with his request—he wanted her to live. She glanced back down the hall and cried upon spotting Nico behind them.

As he spotted the killer running towards them, Stephen shoved Charlene again and yelled, "Go!"

Charlene sobbed as she ran down the hall. She could hear radio chatter near the entrance—the sound of police radios. She heard the sound of footsteps behind her. One set was fast and loud, the other was weak and inconsistent. She didn't stop running, though. She sprinted towards the light at the end of the hallway.

"Get on the ground!" a booming male voice shouted.

Other variations of the same demand echoed down the hall: *Stop! Don't move! Put your hands up!*

Another male officer shouted, "Knife! Knife!"

Upon hearing those words, Charlene knew the confrontation would end in a shooting—they always did. Near the entrance, the young woman fell to the floor with her hands on her head. She tightly closed her eyes as she lay on her stomach, waiting for the inevitable shooting. She winced as the sound of gunfire reverberated through the building.

The police shot into the corridor for ten seconds, but it felt like ten minutes. Twenty rounds sounded more like a thousand.

As the gunfire stopped, Charlene lifted her head from the floor and glanced around. Police officers moved in front of her, but the noise was muffled. She glanced back into the hallway. Nico lay near a set of lockers. He appeared to be screaming, but he was neutralized by the gunfire. Stephen lay near the lockers across the hall from the killer. He held his leg up and screamed at the top of his lungs. He was hit by a stray bullet—*collateral damage.*

Charlene turned back towards the main entrance. Two police officers lifted her from the ground. She could finally hear the sound of chaos—and it was deafening.

***

Charlene sat in the passenger seat of a police cruiser, a fleece blanket draped over her shoulders. She watched as police officers, detectives, forensic specialists, and paramedics wandered the area. The process was methodical—some gathered evidence, others helped the survivors, and all of them worked in perfect harmony.

The young woman turned her attention to the windshield. An ambulance was parked in front of the police cruiser. Due to the severity of his wounds, Nico was being loaded into the wagon. The killer was going to spend a few nights in the hospital instead of jail. The ambulance reminded her of Stephen, though. The stoner was already taken away in another ambulance. *Are you okay? Did you survive?*–she thought.

Charlene snapped out of her contemplation as the door beside her swung open. She smiled at her savior—Sheriff Cameron Jackson. Jackson returned the smile and nodded.

He said, "I'm sorry to keep you waiting, miss. It's just part of the... the job." He glanced over at the ambulance, despondent. He asked, "Are you sure you don't need any medical assistance? It wouldn't hurt to get checked out, right?"

Charlene shook her head and said, "No. I'm fine, really. I just want to go home. I want to go to bed. I want to sleep. I just want to get away from this nightmare."

"Unfortunately, you won't be going home right away. We're going to have to take you down to the station to ask you some questions. We just want to get your side of the story as soon as possible. Then, we'll send you home with your parents."

Charlene bit her bottom lip and stared down at her lap. She escaped from the school, unscathed and informed, but she was still trapped in the nightmare. She didn't expect to escape from her nightmare anytime soon, either. The massacre clung to her mind, poisoning her every thought.

As she blankly stared at the dashboard, Charlene asked, "Do you have any idea what happened in there?"

Jackson said, "Yeah, we have an idea. Our suspect, Nico Marshall, wanted to kill you and your friends. Unfortunately, under my watch, he mostly succeeded."

He sighed and stared down at his boots. Guilt festered in his heart, tormenting him. He sought to protect and serve, but he felt like he harmed and neglected his community instead.

The sheriff said, "I'm sorry about that. We tried our best to stop this from happening. It just felt like... like we were sent on a wild-goose chase. Things just didn't add up, but we still tried to force it." As the ambulance drove away from the school, Jackson said, "One thing is for certain: the killer has been caught and this nightmare has ended."

It's just getting started—Charlene bit her tongue before she could blurt the blunt response. The sheriff was genuine. His sincerity was comforting during the chaotic time. She didn't want to agitate him by placing more guilt on his shoulders.

Charlene said, "Nico did this for his brother. I don't know if you remember it, but a kid named Casey Marshall killed himself a year ago—maybe it was a year and a half. He killed himself because he was being bullied. Nico was just getting vengeance and my boyfriend, Adam, helped him. I didn't know about it. I swear, I would have said something if I knew. I-"

Charlene stopped. She furrowed her brow and

tilted her head as she stared off into space. She remembered Nico's rant. She wasn't accused of bullying Casey, but she was scolded for her apathetic negligence. She didn't tell the faculty about Casey's bullying, so she wondered if she really would have told the police about Nico and Adam if she had found out about them earlier.

Jackson patted her shoulder and said, "Don't dwell on it, miss. None of this is your fault. I'd like to hear everything you have to say, but maybe we should wait until we're at the station. We can get you some coffee or water when we arrive. Let's–"

"Jackson!" a police officer interrupted as he approached the sheriff. The officer said, "Jackson, mount up. We're in pursuit of two suspects—possibly three—who escaped the school through the rear exit. Miller said they were wearing raincoats. They hopped into a black sedan and they may be heading towards Kamala."

"More suspects?" Jackson whispered, shocked. He hit the hood of the police cruiser and said, "Get her to the station. I'll go with Webb. Go!"

As Jackson slammed the door in her face, Charlene tapped the window and cried, "I don't know who they are! Be careful! They killed my friends! Please... be careful."

She watched as the sheriff sprinted towards a police cruiser in the parking lot to join another officer in the pursuit. She was amazed by the cops' bravery.

Another officer sat in the driver's seat beside Charlene. The officer offered some words of comfort to the traumatized student. Charlene didn't hear his words, though. She remembered Britney's text message, which revealed a third party in the attack. She could only think about the killers and the victims as the car rolled away from the school.

Chapter Twenty-One

Tragedy Begets Tragedy

Police cars surrounded a one-story house in a suburban neighborhood, blue and red lights blinking. The front door of the house was left open, swinging in the doorway. A black sedan was parked on the front lawn, driver and passenger doors open.

Jackson, along with five other officers, lined up beside the house. The sheriff stood at the back of the line while the officer at the front led the way with a ballistic shield. Weapons drawn, the officers held each other's shoulders.

As they marched into the house, Jackson shouted, "Police! Stay where you are! Police!"

Police, don't move, keep your hands up—the words echoed through the home as the officers screamed different variations of the same statement: *comply or die.* The police moved swiftly, shouting their positions while individually clearing the rooms in the house. They were not met with any resistance, though. Although the door was open and the car was parked on the lawn, the home appeared to be empty.

Jackson pulled away from the group in the living room, shocked. The furniture was overturned and damaged. The glass coffee table was shattered into a hundred pieces. The end-tables and the sofas were flipped. The sofa cushions were shredded. The large flat-screen television was broken, cracked as if something were hurled at it. A lamp on the floor, likely knocked over from one of the end-tables, illuminated most of the room. The destruction was surprising. On the other hand, the blood on the walls was terrifying.

As if a child were using the house as a canvas for his finger-painting, large messages were scrawled on the walls in blood. One message read: *Egos lead to ignorance.* The message below it read: *Ignorance leads to hatred.* The next message read: *Hatred leads to tragedy.* Above the archway leading to the kitchen, the final message read: *Tragedy creates tragedy*

Jackson strolled through the archway and entered the kitchen. The floor was flooded with shards from broken plates and cups. He couldn't take a single step without crushing a shard. Blood stained the countertops and floor, streaming across the drawers and cupboards. The cupboards appeared to be punched through the center. The kitchen table and the chairs were also overturned and broken.

As he examined the damage, Jackson whispered, "What the hell happened here?"

Jackson, visibly rattled by the discovery, returned to the living room. He walked through an archway on the other side of the room and found himself in a hallway. His team was clearing the rooms at the end of the hall. Still, they didn't find any resistance in the house.

The sheriff opened the first door to his left. Like the living room and kitchen, the furniture in the bedroom was overturned and broken. The drawers from the dresser were pulled out and tossed onto the floor. The mirror attached to the dresser was shattered, blood dripping across the glass.

Judging from the pink walls and the photos of girls in the room, Jackson assumed the bedroom belonged to a teenage girl. He closed the room, then he proceeded to the second door to the left. He opened the door and stood in the doorway, baffled.

Yet again, the room was destroyed. The dresser drawers were tossed on the floor, overturned and broken. Clothing flooded the floor, too. The clothing appeared wet and heavy, though. From the pungent scent lingering in the room, it was safe to assume the clothing was drenched in urine. Gaping holes were punched into the walls. An angry, malevolent aura lingered in the room.

From the neighboring room, an officer said, "Jackson, check this out."

Jackson took one final glance at the bedroom, then he joined his partner at the neighboring room —the bathroom. Jackson stood in the doorway while his partner stood in front of the toilet. The man appeared confused—a furrowed brow and an open mouth.

Jackson asked, "What is it?"

The officer responded, "The toilet... It's clogged."

"So?"

"Look. It's clogged with... with shredded money."

Jackson stepped into the room, curious. He stood beside his partner and stared into the toilet. Indeed, the bowl was filled to the brim with shredded cash and water. There wasn't a single bill under one-hundred dollars, either. Thousands of dollars were flushed down the drain. *It means something,* the sheriff thought, *what were they trying to say?*

Stony-faced, the sheriff walked out of the

bathroom. He stood in the hallway, lost in his thoughts. He thought about the destruction and the messages in the living room, but he couldn't link the pieces. He staggered towards the last door to the left while the rest of his partners huddled around the last door to the right.

As he reached the bedroom, Jackson leaned on the doorway and sighed—disoriented by the revelation. The dark room was not destroyed. In fact, there wasn't a single speck of dust in the bedroom. It looked as if it had not been modified in over a year—trapped in time. The cleanliness of the room did not catch the sheriff off guard, though.

The walls were decorated with dozens of homemade paper-mâché masks. All of the masks, regardless of design, were painted with smeared makeup. All of the masks also shared the same bloody tears. The pieces were easy to link: the room belonged to Casey Marshall and his masks were used during the murders.

Jackson whispered, "She was right... Christ, she was right..."

He walked back into the hall. He stopped as he bumped into one of the officers crowding the parallel room—the last room on the right. The cops turned towards each other and locked eyes. They both appeared horrified and confused. The sheriff had a reason for being frightened, but he didn't know the officer's excuse.

Jackson pushed his way past the cops and stared into the last bedroom. He froze with fear as he examined the room. Three people lay on a queen-sized bed, as if they were cuddling for warmth. He recognized them, too.

Nicholas Marshall, Casey's father, lay on the center of the mattress. Abigail Marshall, Casey's mother, lay to the man's left, her head resting on his shoulder. Bethany Marshall, Casey's teenage sister, lay to the man's right, her head resting on her father's sturdy chest. The family wore matching raincoats, pants, and boots, but they no longer wore their masks. The family lay motionless, eyes closed as if they had fallen asleep. They weren't sleeping, though.

They were dead.

Sleeves pushed up to their elbows, their forearms and wrists were drenched in blood. They cut their wrists vertically across their veins. It was a family suicide. On the wall above the bed, written in blood, a message read: *For Casey.*

Holding his hand over his mouth, Jackson approached the bed. The poignant portrait of suicide was depressing. Protocol dictated his actions, but he was unable to move forward. *A family that kills together dies together*—he had never seen anything like it before.

He glanced over his shoulder. A laptop sat on top of the dresser across from the foot of the bed. The laptop was open and powered on. The family live-streamed their suicide on Facebook—and the stream was active with an audience of thousands. Some of the viewers were concerned, others were apathetic, and a few posted some stale internet jokes. None of the viewers seemed concerned with reporting the tragedy. People were attracted to the macabre.

Jackson sighed in disappointment, then he closed the laptop.

Chapter Twenty-Two

Closure

Charlene sat in Sheriff Jackson's office, hunched forward with her shoulders pulled in tight towards her chest. She vacantly stared down at her shoes, brooding over the tragedy. Jackson sat across from her, scribbling on a sheet of paper. He was only trying to buy himself some time to think, though.

The sheriff placed the pen down, then he clasped his hands under his chin. He said, "Thank you for your patience, Ms. Sanchez. I know it's been a long night. Don't worry, I won't be asking you any other questions. Not now, at least. This is... This is time that I set aside for you. You deserve closure from me —not Channel 5 News, MSNBC, CNN. You deserve to hear it from *me.* I was responsible for this case and... and I feel partly responsible for what you experienced. So, if you have any questions, I'm all ears."

Charlene slowly lifted her head and stared up at the sheriff. She could see the guilt in his eyes. She could also see he was sincere about his offer. He was breaking procedure, but he felt compelled to comfort the young woman.

Charlene asked, "So, you found out what happened? It was 'cause of Casey, right?"

"Yes, we believe so. Nico and his accomplices set out to kill the people they believed were responsible for Casey's death."

"Accomplices... You're talking about Adam, right? You found his phone? His messages? You have proof, right?"

Jackson nodded and said, "You were correct. He was sending messages to Nico and Nico was informing his family."

Charlene furrowed her brow and repeated, "*His family?*"

"Yes. That's the reason we didn't stop them sooner. Nico and Adam weren't working alone. Nico's parents and even his sister helped him. It's completely possible that they each killed at least one person. So, at one point, we were looking for a man like Nico or Nicholas, his dad. Then, we found long hair in Melanie's home and that didn't belong to Melanie or her mother. This conflicting evidence sent us in circles. One moment, we were hunting a man; the next, we were looking for a woman. We were foolish, Ms. Sanchez. We should have been looking for a family..."

Charlene breathed heavily as she leaned back in her seat. She was flabbergasted by the information. *A family of killers,* she thought, *who would have suspected all of them?*

She said, "Well, um... I'm... I'm glad it's over. I hope you send Nico away for a long time."

"We will. You have my word."

"I have to ask: are... are all of my friends dead? Did Britney make it? How about Dominique? I didn't see them die. Did they... Did they die?"

Jackson sighed, then he said, "Unfortunately, your friends passed away. Dominique, Britney, Adam, and the teacher, Mr. Collin Wilson, were found dead at the scene. We couldn't revive them. I'm sorry."

Tears streamed across Charlene's cheeks as she blinked. At heart, she already knew her friends were dead. She figured she would have seen them at the station if they survived. She was prepared to hear the truth, though.

She sniffled and said, "Stephen... What about Stephen? He was with me when we were in the hallway."

"He's at the hospital now. I believe he was in stable condition the last time we checked. I don't want to promise anything, but I think he's going to be fine. He'll recover. He's a strong kid."

Despite the night of murder, Charlene cracked a smile. She couldn't help but laugh, too—laughter of relief. She lost some of her closest friends, but she was pleased to hear her rescuer, the young man who risked everything for her, survived.

Jackson said, "I would just like to apologize, Ms. Sanchez. If we only worked faster, if we only saw the signs, then maybe things would have turned out differently. You went through hell—and you're still not out. We'll be here for you, though."

Charlene coughed and grunted, trying to choke back her tears. She stuttered, "Th–Thank you. I... I don't want you to feel guilty for doing your job, though. You did what you had to do. I think it's... it's our fault anyway. I didn't bully Casey. I didn't even know the kid. I knew who he was, but we never said a word to each other. I saw the bullying, though, and I heard all about it. I didn't help by staying quiet. If I told someone—a counselor or the principal—this probably would have never happened."

"You shouldn't feel guilty, either, miss. I believe you're a good person. This experience might have torn you apart and brought you to your knees, but, when you get up, you'll be a better person. So will I. I believe we can do more to curb bullying in school and social media. We've seen what bullying can do first-hand, so hopefully we can start preventing it."

Charlene nodded in agreement. At that moment, she vowed to fight against bullying. She would avenge Casey using a humane method.

Jackson smiled and said, "You can go home now, Ms. Sanchez. I believe your parents are still waiting right outside. Have a good night. You have my number. Call me if you need anything."

"Thank you. Thank you for everything."

Charlene exited the room and closed the door behind her. She glanced down the hall to her right. Her parents stood at the end of the hall, arm-in-arm. Her mother sobbed into a napkin while her father tried to crack a smile. They were relieved. The teenager couldn't keep her facade afloat. She was a strong person, a fighter and a survivor, but she couldn't contain herself. She grimaced and cried, overwhelmed by her emotions. She lurched into her parents' arms, happy to feel their embrace.

Charlene was simultaneously coddled and scolded by her parents. She couldn't hear a single word, though. She could feel their love and concern, but she couldn't hear them. The world around her was muted. She could only think about Nico, Casey, and her friends. After the massacre at the school, she was just happy to be alive.

Join the mailing list!

Did you enjoy the book? Do you need more horror in your life? I have good news for you: I release horror books on a *monthly* basis. I release dark, disturbing horror novels and throwback slashers—and everything in between, including psychological and supernatural horror. By signing up for my mailing list, you'll be the first to know about new books, deep discounts, and free books. Best of all, it requires very little effort on your part— and it's free! Oh, and you'll only receive 1-2 emails per month. Visit this link to sign-up: http://eepurl.com/bNl1CP

Dear Reader,

Hello! Thanks for reading *The Social Media Murders.* This was a whodunit/slasher hybrid—at least, that's what I wanted to create. Since it was also an *extreme* horror book, there were some very violent deaths. The book also featured themes of bullying and suicide. I know these are very sensitive subjects. If you were offended by the contents of this book, please accept my sincerest apologies. As usual, I never intended on offending anyone.

Like I already stated, *The Social Media Murders* is a whodunit-slasher novel. It was mainly inspired by Wes Craven's *Scream* and Dario Argento's classic horror movies. I even mention Argento in the first chapter. Actually, I mentioned *Scream* a few times, too. I'm a big fan of Wes Craven and Dario Argento, so I wanted to create something similar. Of course, I'm not restricted by the MPAA or some big publisher, so I was free to create some *very* brutal death scenes, including a few jaw-ripping scenes.

Aside from my love for slashers, the film was also inspired by social media. If you've seen me on Twitter or Facebook, you know I'm not an outspoken person. That's because I'm naturally a bashful guy. I don't mind talking to people, though, and I don't mind sharing my opinions on things. In fact, I like social media. I think it's a great way to connect and share; it opens doors to places we might have never seen otherwise.

However, there is a dark side to social media—and that's what inspired this book. These days, people use social media to complain, argue, bully, and even *murder.* It seems to be snowballing out of control, too. It feels like someone uses social media for something worse every month. And, a lot of people do it just for 'likes.' I wanted to target that obsession to social media—and the flaws that accompany these types of websites—with this book. Now, I only hope someone doesn't use social media to become a serial killer or to post his murders online. I've had some bad timing with some of my previous books reflecting some horrendous *real-life* crimes.

The first draft of this book was completed in January 2017. I know some things have happened since then regarding social media and live-streamed murders, but I just want to note: this was *not* meant to glorify these criminals. I know it's called *The Social Media Murders,* but that title was inspired by the title for the 1978 film *The Toolbox Murders.* This novel wasn't based on any real events. Okay?

Anyway, if you enjoyed this book, I'd *really* appreciate it if you left a review on Amazon.com. Your review will help me improve on my writing and it will help me gain visibility on Amazon. If more people read my books, then I can write *more* for everyone. So, if you're a fan of my writing, reviews will help me release books more frequently. And, it will only take you five or so minutes to write a review. Do you like my slasher novels? Would you like to read more? If so, what type of slasher would you like me to write? Or, would you like me to stick to the darker books I've written in the past? Would you read another book like this in the future? Answering questions like these will allow me to better understand you, the reader. Your words have the power to influence my writing—please use them wisely.

Feel free to share this book with your friends and family. This book is about social media, so share it on social media. Tweet it on Twitter, share it with your friends and family on Facebook, or... What else do all of you use? I don't know, just spread the word. You can even buy a copy for a friend. Word-of-mouth is a superb method in supporting independent authors —and it's mostly *free.*

This may come as a surprise to you, but: I'm *still* not a bestselling author. Shocking, isn't it? Still, I really appreciate your support. As long as you keep reading, I can keep writing. Thank you for giving me this opportunity.

Finally, if you enjoy scary stories, feel free to visit my Amazon's Author page. I've published over a dozen horror novels as well as some science-fiction/fantasy books. If you want to read a psychological horror novel, check out *Madness at Madison Mall.* If you're looking for a brutal revenge thriller/horror book, check out my upcoming book, *The Law of Retaliation*—it should be out in August 2017. Keep your eyes peeled for my upcoming books since I release a new book every month. Feel free to check out my older novels in the meantime. I really appreciate it! Once again, thank you for reading. Your readership keeps me going through the darkest times!

Until our next venture into the dark and disturbing,
Jon Athan

P.S. If you have questions (or insults), you can contact me via Twitter @Jonny_Athan, or my Facebook page, or through my business email: info@jon-athan.com. If you're an aspiring author, I'm always happy to offer a helping hand. Even if you have a simple question, don't hesitate to contact me. Thanks again!

Printed in Great Britain
by Amazon